AS SHE FADES

AS SHE FADES

ABBI GLINES

FEIWEL AND FRIENDS

NEW YORK

A FEIWEL AND FRIENDS BOOK
An imprint of Macmillan Publishing Group, LLC
175 Fifth Avenue, New York, NY 10010

Our books may be purchased in bulk for promotional, educational, or business use.
Please contact your local bookseller or the Macmillan Corporate and Premium Sales
Department at (800) 221-7945 ext. 5442 or by e-mail at MacmillanSpecialMarkets@
macmillan.com.

Library of Congress Control Number: 2017944809

ISBN 978-1-250-13386-1 (hardcover) / ISBN 978-1-250-13387-8 (ebook)

Book design by Danielle Mazzella di Bosco
Feiwel and Friends logo designed by Filomena Tuosto

First edition, 2018

10 9 8 7 6 5 4 3 2 1

fiercereads.com

For every girl who has been broken
and found her strength to fight

PART ONE

Take this kiss upon the brow!
And, in parting from you now,
Thus much let me avow—
You are not wrong, who deem
That my days have been a dream;
Yet if hope has flown away
In a night, or in a day,
In a vision, or in none,
Is it therefore the less *gone*?
All that we see or seem
Is but a dream within a dream.

—Edgar Allan Poe, "A Dream Within a Dream"

SINCE I WAS a little girl, I've loved fairy tales. And I've believed in true love. It was easy for me, though, because I fell in love at six years old. Not many people find love so young. Crawford and I believed we were special. That fate shined on us and gave us each other early so we'd have a lifetime together. He was my very own Prince Charming. Not one day of my childhood was he not there with me. Making me smile and enjoying the life we were both born into. But what we didn't expect were the sharp turns in life you don't see coming. The ones that knock you off course. The things that come along and change it all forever. We hadn't been prepared for that.

OUR STORY ISN'T an easy one. The charmed life we had grown up with was pulled away from us so quickly, we didn't have time to prepare for it. But no one ever does. That's the dark side of life.

CHAPTER ONE

THE SMELL OF summer evenings always made me feel happy. Since I was a girl, it was the reminder that school was over and adventure awaited. Swimming in the lake, playing basketball with my older brothers, and of course our annual family vacation. However, this year it meant freedom. A new life, a new beginning. For me and Crawford.

I glanced over at him driving and the warmth in my chest grew at the sight of him. We had been together since we were kids. First as friends, and then it grew into more as we got older. Today we had walked across the large stage set in the center of our high school football field and received our diplomas. We were graduates. Finally.

"Still seems hard to believe it's over. High school," I added for clarification. Although I was sure he would understand what I meant.

He cut his eyes toward me and the corner of his lips curved up just enough for his eyes to sparkle the way they did when he was amused or pleased. "It's not over. It's just beginning, V. Our life will be exactly like we planned it."

I wanted to believe that. We were going to the same college. Crawford had a scholarship for football. A full ride. It wasn't my first choice for school but I wanted to be where he was. We had never been apart.

"Everyone seemed almost scared tonight. Like they were drinking and partying to forget the fact we're adults now. This is it."

Crawford shrugged. "I bet most of them are terrified. They don't all have plans like we do. They have to decide what's next."

He was right, of course. He always was. One of the things I loved about Crawford was his confidence. He didn't worry and back away from a problem. He faced it head-on and took control. I felt safe with him, like he would always have the answer I needed.

His hand reached over and covered mine. "Our life is going to be amazing. College is going to be just what we need. To get out of this town but not too far away. We can spread our wings and still come home to visit easily enough. You're going to love it."

And I believed him. My mind was playing through all the fun things we would see and do. Excitement for what was to come bubbled up in me and I was so ready for August to arrive.

Our favorite song came on the radio and Crawford turned it up and began to sing along with his off-key voice. He was a terrible singer, but he knew it made me laugh so he did it often. Joy swelled up in me for the life I had, so strong it was hard to contain it. I began to laugh as he hit another bad note. This was my life and I loved it.

It was then that Crawford slammed on the brakes and the world began spinning. The smell of burning rubber and the violent screeching of wheels took away all my other thoughts. Dreams vanished in that instant. Completely.

• • •

ONE MONTH. TODAY was the one-month anniversary of the car accident that turned our graduation night into a nightmare. I sat in the waiting room—now more familiar to me than my own bedroom—and stared at the white walls. The smell of stale coffee didn't overpower the sterile surroundings. Those things didn't matter, though. Nothing other than Crawford opening his eyes mattered.

It would be my turn to read to Crawford soon. I lived for this time of day. To see him and pray he would hear my voice and open his eyes. That we would be together again. That all our dreams were still there, waiting just outside the door of this lonely, cold place.

The doctor had told his parents the morning after the accident that he believed comatose patients can hear. If he heard us talking to him, he'd fight to come back. To wake up.

I shivered remembering those words. *Comatose.* I hated that. Crawford was so full of life and energy. Seeing him like this was so hard.

The doctor believed he needed to hear several voices he knew and loved. So Crawford's mother put us on a schedule in the beginning, but then let me come in as early as I wanted to read. But as the days progressed, her schedule had started to change as her health went downhill. Seeing her only child like this day in and day out was weighing on her.

"Still here?" a masculine voice asked. I didn't recognize the speaker. Normally it was one of my older brothers coming to check on me. Knox, my youngest older brother, was closest in age to Crawford and me, and he came to read, too. Not every day like me, but when he could. I was hoping he would come today. He hadn't been in a couple of days and I knew Crawford would like to hear him.

I lifted my head to meet a pair of dark green eyes outlined by thick black lashes—pretty eyes for a guy. I'd seen those eyes before. Just as I'd seen the guy they belonged to. But we had never spoken.

"You're always here," he said. "There hasn't been a day in the past two weeks that I've not seen you."

His voice was smooth, but there was a thicker drawl to his accent than most of the guys had in Franklin. He almost sounded Alabama-ish. Was he studying me or was he waiting on me to speak? Probably the latter. I was being rude not responding.

"Nowhere else to be," I said honestly. Because without Crawford I was lost.

He lifted the corner of his full lips and it looked a lot like a smirk. Why would he be smirking at something like this?

"I can think of a lot of places I'd rather be. But Uncle D is where my loyalty lies. So here I am."

I wasn't sure if he meant to be deep and heartfelt, but it didn't sound that way. I wondered if he was even upset about his uncle being here. Not that it was my business. The guy had an air about him that rubbed me the wrong way. He liked himself. A lot. He knew he was beautiful and he liked the attention it got him. I'd seen his kind plenty. I wasn't a fan.

"Your selflessness humbles me," I replied with a heavy dash of sarcasm. The way his eyes sparked with amusement made me dislike him more than I'd already decided I did.

As he crossed his arms over his wide chest, I couldn't help but notice the way his biceps flexed and the tattoo peeking out of his sleeve. His long dark hair was a little messy and tucked behind his ears. I imagined it would complete his pirate look if he had it pulled back in a ponytail.

"Don't mistake me for pretending to be selfless. That was never my intention at all. I'm here to see my uncle. Nothing deeper than that. But then, I don't sit like a martyr in this waiting room day after day and stare at that wall. Selflessness is your thing. Not mine."

Why was he still talking to me? Where was Knox? He should have showed up with a late lunch from my mom by now. And it was his turn to go sit with Crawford before my scheduled time in three hours. Knox needed to get here and this guy needed to move on along.

"Jesus, you're high-strung," he muttered, and I jerked my gaze back to his. Again with that amused smile.

"Aren't you here to see your uncle?" I asked, hoping to get rid of him.

He laughed this time. The real kind. It was pleasant. Maybe more than pleasant. Until I remembered he was laughing in that attractive way because of me. Then it annoyed me.

"I am. Just thought I'd try and give you something to do other than stare at the wall. It makes me sad when I see you here all alone. My mistake. You're obviously alone because you like it that way."

I would not rise to the bait. He wanted me to bite back, but I wasn't going to do it. He wasn't worth my anger or the energy it would take to get angry.

"Slate, what are you doing out here? Your uncle was just asking about you." The young female nurse was seriously batting her eyelashes and sticking out her chest as she spoke to . . . *Slate*—apparently that was his name.

He turned his gaze to meet hers and I was almost positive he winked. Her cheeks began to glow and her eyes went all sultry. *Jesus.* I had seen enough of this. If I wanted to watch a soap opera, I'd turn on the television in the corner.

"Tell the old man I'm coming," he said.

She giggled like that was hilarious and gave me a brief glance before turning to walk away. The swing in her hips was exaggerated—any girl who actually walked like that would need to get her hips adjusted at the chiropractor weekly.

"You enjoy yourself, Miss . . ." He trailed off, as if waiting on me to give him my name. He would be waiting forever.

"Your fan club needs you," I replied with a disgusted tone, and went back to staring at the wall. Just like I did every day. Thinking. About life and my future, our future. Mine and Crawford's.

"Yeah, it does." He chuckled. Out of the corner of my eye, I saw him shake his head before turning and walking away. It wasn't a walk, really. More of a saunter. If guys actually sauntered. Maybe a swagger?

Oh, who cared? He was gone.

I reached into my canvas tote bag and pulled out my phone. There were five texts and two calls from my mother, a text from each of my four brothers, two from my oldest brother's wife, and the last three from my dad. They did this every day. Checking on me, asking me to come to dinner, a movie, shopping, to play basketball . . . anything to try to get me out of this hospital.

None of them understood. Crawford was in a coma.

That was all that mattered. I couldn't just continue to live as if he weren't lying in that bed, unmoving. I had to be here when he woke up. Because he would. He *had* to. We had a future we'd been planning since childhood.

I opened my text messages and did what any good girl would do: I began replying to them. My mother's offer to take me shopping for a new bathing suit—as if I were going to the beach anytime soon. Then her attempt to guilt me into a family dinner. My nieces missed me. I did feel slightly guilty about Maddy and Malyn, my oldest brother's twin girls. They were only two, and Aunt Vale not being around probably confused them.

Before the accident, I babysat them every Tuesday and Thursday night while Catherine, my sister-in-law, worked late shifts at the nursing home. My mom kept them now. I wouldn't leave the hospital each day until I had to. When Crawford's mother came back at seven every evening, I told him good night, kissed his cheek, then cried the whole way home. When I woke up at seven every morning, I got dressed, packed my bag with books and snacks, and headed to the hospital. It was my routine. It was all I had left.

My brothers were getting together tonight after family dinner to play basketball at the house. Jonah was in the military and currently on assignment. So I was the even number four. They didn't really need me. My dad would be there to fill in. But each of them acted like they couldn't play without me.

I was the baby of the five and the only girl. That being said, I was also overprotected and worried about too much. They all thought it was their job to make sure I was okay. Because I loved them each for it, and because Jonah texted me even while he was off serving our country, I replied to all of them that I'd be at the basketball game if they'd wait until seven thirty. It wasn't what I wanted to do when I got home. But it was what they needed me to do.

So I'd do it.

CHAPTER TWO

KNOX ARRIVED, FINALLY. He held a blue polka-dot lunchbox that I knew would be filled with a hot meal. This was how my mother kept her sanity with my staying up here all day—she kept me fed.

"Here you go, Princess." Knox handed over the lunchbox and sank down into the chair next to me. "How's it going?"

He usually stayed and talked to me while I ate. It was something I looked forward to. Knox was only two years older than me and we were the closest out of the five of us.

He had my dark hair and blue eyes. Everyone said we could have been twins.

"Same. Just waiting," I replied. "How's the home front?"

He sighed and leaned back in his chair, crossing his arms over his chest. "Dad's fighting with the plumber over the price of the new tub Momma wants, Momma is making your favorite cake in hopes she can lure you home for dinner, and Maddy refuses to use the big-girl potty because Aunt Vale isn't there to sing the potty song to her."

He wasn't trying to make me feel guilty. That wasn't Knox's style. He was just being honest.

"Can't Mom sing the song to her? She's the one who taught it to me." I pulled out a container of broccoli casserole. It was still nice and warm.

He shrugged. "She tried. Maddy said it wasn't like yours."

I had to find time to see my nieces. "I wish Mom would bring them here to see me."

Knox turned his head to look at me. "Why? You're not in a hospital bed. You can walk out anytime you want and do other things. Crawford would want you to."

Again, he wasn't being cruel. But Knox's honesty was sometimes brutal.

"When he opens his eyes I want to be here," I said for the hundredth time. It was something they all knew, but I kept having to repeat it.

"He could wake up in the middle of the night. You're not here then."

I knew that. I hated it. But I wasn't allowed to sleep in the waiting room. When visiting hours were over I had to leave. Hospital rules. I'd tried it already. They'd kicked me out.

"Just let me do this my way," I said, then took a bite of my lunch. I was hungry. My breakfast of dry cereal and goldfish crackers was long gone and I needed something other than stale coffee.

"Knox McKinley," a now-familiar male voice said, and I almost choked on my casserole, which made me want to cuss. Did that asshole have to know my brother?

"Slate," Knox replied with a smile in his voice that was real. He liked this guy. Go figure. "What are you doing here?"

"I was about to ask you the same. I see you made more headway with that one than I did. She would rather stare at the wall than speak to me."

I felt Knox turn to look at me, but I ignored them both and took a bite of my food. This was not how I'd hoped to enjoy my meal.

"Yeah, well, I bring her food and share the same parents, so she has to speak to me," Knox replied.

"She's your sister. That helps my ego somewhat."

I pulled out the yeast roll I knew my momma had made fresh and took a large bite. One too big to be expected to speak. I heard Knox muffle a laugh. Maybe he'd get the hint and send Mr. Annoying on his way.

"I thought you lived in Huntsville with your uncle? What brings you this far out?"

Knox was changing the subject. I owed him one for that.

"Uncle D has stage four cancer. It's in his liver. This is the closest hospital equipped to handle that."

Oh. The uncle he lived with was dying. Now I felt a little bad. Okay, maybe a lot bad.

"I'm sorry—I hadn't heard anything about it before summer break." Knox was sincere. He had a big heart.

"He didn't tell me about it until I got home. Then he had his first surgery two weeks ago. Once he's recovered he'll start chemo. All they're promising is that it'll prolong his life. Not save it."

"Damn," Knox whispered, and shook his head. "Well, if there's anything I can do, let me know. I bring my sister lunch daily. I can do the same for you if you need it." Knox again meant every word. He'd have our momma making this guy meals starting tomorrow.

"Nah, I don't camp out up here. Uncle D would be pissed if I tried. I stop by once or twice a day. I've got a friend in town and I'm crashing at her place."

That was more like it. Crashing at a girl's place. No wonder he didn't stay with his uncle. He had a female to get to.

"Okay, well, if you need something you got my number."

"Thanks, man."

"Brothers," Knox said, then did that hand thing I recognized as Kappa Sigma. They were fraternity brothers.

"See you around. Keep that friendly sister of yours under control." Slate's voice was teasing, and I swallowed my roll before glancing up at him. He winked and I turned my attention back to my food.

"I'll do my best."

Once he was gone Knox looked at me. "Smart girl."

I frowned and turned my gaze to his. I was expecting to get scolded for dissing his frat brother. "What?"

Knox nodded at Slate's retreating form. "Blowing him off. He's my brother and he's a great guy, but he's a slut. I'd wager he's slept with every hot nurse on this floor already. The guy gets around. He's a legend in Kappa Sigma."

That, I did not have to be told. "I already had him figured out."

Knox patted my knee. "I should have known."

Yeah, he should've.

CHAPTER THREE

CRAWFORD'S MOTHER, JULIET, had been like a second mother to me most of my life. She was younger than my mom and Crawford was her only child. She had married his father right out of high school and completely believed in young love being strong enough to last the test of time.

However, over the past month she had changed. The vibrant, smiling woman was no more. She had wrinkles now I hadn't noticed before. Her once-gorgeous blond hair was thin and brittle. Her shoulders slumped forward all the time where once she had stood tall with excellent posture and poise.

Crawford was her world, too. She was falling apart without him and I understood. I accepted her sharp words and strict rules about visitation. I didn't let my feelings get hurt when she complained about my always sitting in the waiting room. She was hurting and she needed to lash out. I was here to take it. Crawford would do the same for me.

I recognized the click of her heels just as the hands on the clock I'd been watching for over an hour moved into the four o'clock position. She was leaving to go home to eat, bathe, and rest before coming back to stay the night. She refused to let her husband or me stay. She had to be here. In case.

In case he opened his eyes. Or . . . he didn't.

I waited until she appeared in the doorway to wave me over. It was our routine and I followed it. She needed that control. I picked up my bag and stood. It was my turn with Crawford, finally.

"He's had a bit more brain activity today. Knox coming in and reading to him the short time he did was good for him, I think. If anything changes call me immediately," Juliet said. Normally that would be good news, but it was what she had been saying every day for the past month.

"I will," I assured her.

She nodded and glanced back at his door one more time before squeezing my shoulder and walking away.

This was the only part of my day I looked forward to yet dreaded just the same. Seeing Crawford hooked up to those machines with his eyes closed never got easier. The pain was always there. Just as strong as it was the night he ran the new stop sign on County Road 14 and a truck T-boned us on Crawford's side going fifty miles an hour. I hadn't even lost consciousness. I remembered every moment of it. Screaming his name as his lifeless body lay there. Unable to free him or even open my door. Blood from the gash in my head dripped into my eyes, blurring my vision, but I had witnessed it all. Every terrifying second.

The only mark I had left from that night was the scar from the stitches just under my hairline. My bruises had long since healed. The concussion was also gone. It wasn't fair that he was the one lying there. I'd been laughing as he sang off-key to a song and he'd glanced over to smile at me. That had been the last thing I saw before we flipped several times and metal screeched and the stench of burning rubber filled the air.

Stepping into the room, I let my gaze go directly to Crawford. He was thinner than I'd ever seen him, but the bruises and gashes on his face had healed. He didn't seem so beaten and broken anymore. Just peacefully sleeping and in need of a double cheeseburger.

He loved double cheeseburgers with extra pickles and mustard. I couldn't even bring myself to look at one now. Not without him.

"I'm here. I've got a new book. One that is light on the romance and heavy on the action. Your mom seemed positive about your progress today. I like seeing her happy."

That was a lie. She was far from happy, but if he could hear me I didn't want him worrying about his mom. He always did.

"Knox brought me broccoli casserole and fried chicken. Momma's specialty. I think she's trying to make me fat. He said he read to you from the college sports website you love so much. I'm sure he had a lot of opinions he threw in."

I talked about everything that happened during the day, hoping he could hear me. I liked to think he'd open his eyes to ask me questions if he was curious enough. Several nights a week I'd dream he opened his eyes as I read to him or held his hand. Then when I finally woke up, I'd cry because dreaming didn't make it real. My heart was empty with him not smiling back at me. I was lost, and I would stay that way until he opened his eyes.

For a moment, I thought about telling him about Slate. That had been the only unusual thing that happened today. Except that another patient, Mr. Wagoner, got to go home. I was going to miss him cruising the halls in his wheelchair. But I knew his kids and grandkids were ready to have him back.

"When I leave tonight I've got a game of basketball with the McKinley boys waiting on me. I need you there to help me take them down. You know how cocky they are."

It had once been me, Crawford, and Knox against Jonah, Michea, and Dylan. The youth against the older ones. It wasn't until Dylan married and moved off that we started having some success. Crawford growing five inches in one summer helped, too. He had gotten as tall as Jonah then, six foot three.

"I have an extra slice of chocolate cream pie from lunch. I think Mom is trying to bribe you to open your eyes with her treats. I know she didn't send it for me."

I had lost weight, too. About seven pounds, and on my five-foot-five frame it looked like a lot. Mom was definitely trying to put weight on me.

My phone dinged and I glanced down at it.

Don't forget the game tonight. The text was from Dylan. He wanted me home for several reasons. Maddy's potty training was just one of them.

I won't, I texted back, then looked back at Crawford.

"I'm ready to have you back. I miss you."

He didn't respond. Not even a flicker.

Tears stung my eyes, and I wiped them away before setting my bag down and settling in the chair beside him. I'd read soon, but for now I just wanted to hold his hand and watch him breathe. Reassure myself that Crawford was in there and he'd come back to me. Soon.

CHAPTER FOUR

"THAT COFFEE IS shit. Here, take this. It's yours."

I had been reading when a cup of coffee that smelled like heaven—definitely not stale hospital coffee—was placed under my nose.

I knew that voice. He was back. The slut. But he had coffee. Good coffee. And I'd been awake since four this morning staring at the ceiling fan in my room. I wanted good coffee.

I took the cup before looking up at him. "Thanks," I all but choked out. That was hard to say to him. But I had been taught good manners. He was being nice because I was Knox's sister. I could accept that.

"You get here early. I'm never here this early. Couldn't sleep last night, so I figured I'd get my day started."

Did him buying me good coffee mean I had to converse with him? Probably so. Besides, his uncle was sick. Where was my compassion?

"How's your uncle?" I asked, since that was the only part of his life I was concerned about. I didn't like to see people lose a loved one.

He shrugged. "Stubborn, mouth of a sailor, mean as fuck, and pretty damn lovable all the same."

That wasn't the answer I had been expecting. But I wondered if anyone ever got a real answer out of this guy.

"So," he continued, "we've had coffee, we share a brother, and we both spend time at this place daily. I think this makes us friends."

"We do not share a brother" was my very quick response.

He chuckled and took a sip of his coffee. "Kappa Sigma would disagree. Brothers for life."

I wanted to roll my eyes but the coffee was delicious, so I didn't.

"Why are you here all the time, Vale?" he asked, surprising me with my name. I had not given him that information.

"How do you know my name?" I snapped.

"We share a brother. Now, what keeps you here staring at this wall?" he asked as he pointed to the wall in front of me that held nothing but a single clock.

"If we share a brother, you should already know that."

"Touché," he replied, then took another sip. "Okay. For argument's sake, we don't share an *actual* brother. I know Knox's taste in beer, cards, and women. I don't know much else. Like I didn't know until yesterday he had a sister. So, can I please know what my new friend does up here all day long?"

I was being difficult. *Why?* This guy was just being nice. So he was a flirt and a man-whore. Did this matter to me? Was I just that judgmental? God, I hoped not.

"My boyfriend is in a coma." Saying it out loud hurt. Like slice-through-your-chest-and-make-it-hard-to-breathe kind of hurt.

"Ouch," he said, as if he felt the pain that was currently shooting through me. "How did it happen?"

I needed to talk about this. It was good for me to tell some-one. To try to accept it. "A car accident the night of graduation. I was in the car, too."

"Fuck," he muttered, and dropped his hand to rest his wrist on his thigh while holding his cup with the same hand. "What's it been—a month now?"

I nodded. It had been a month and a day.

"Why can't you sit in his room? Being out here alone every day seems . . . lonely."

He sure was full of a lot of questions.

"I go in for three hours while his parents take a break. It's my time to read to him."

He leaned forward, resting his elbows on his knees and look-ing at me so that I had to either meet his gaze or stare straight ahead rudely.

"So you just sit here all day doing what?"

I appreciated the good coffee. I really did. It was the best coffee I'd had in a while, but this guy was nosy and I wasn't in the mood to defend myself. If I wanted to sit here all day I could. Not him, not my parents, not my brothers, no one had to understand it. I was doing what I had to do to get by each day. My life was in Crawford's room and I wasn't leaving him.

"Yes," I replied.

He nodded and took another sip of his coffee, then turned his attention to the wall in front of us. "You must really love him."

"I have since I was six years old and he brought me my favor-ite brownie to school and snuck it into my lunchbox." That was more than I'd said about him and our past to anyone since the accident. But it had come out easily.

Slate didn't make fun of me. Instead he smiled. A small smile that made his lips curl up only a little. "That's a nice memory."

Yes, it was. I had millions of those memories.

"Never been in love myself. Don't believe in it. But it's nice to hear someone talk about it who does." He took another long sip of his coffee, then stood.

"I hope your boy opens his eyes soon," he said. "I've got to go see the old man and let him beat me in a game of poker. Makes him feel like he's done something."

I didn't imagine Slate let many people win in this world. He seemed to expect to win it all. Knowing he was letting his uncle beat him made him seem a little more human. That, and the coffee. The coffee was nice.

"Thanks. I needed this," I said, raising the cup a bit.

He winked. "Don't we all." Then he turned and walked down the hall.

I may have watched until he turned left and out of sight. Not that I liked him, but he had a nice walk.

"Someone said Slate Allen was in here." A nurse interrupted my thoughts, which needed interrupting.

So his last name was Allen.

"He just went that way. To his uncle's room," I said, pointing down the hallway.

She grinned brightly. "Thank you!" Then she hurried after him.

That was a different one from the one yesterday. Slate Allen really did get around. The nurses here had to be a couple years older than him, but they didn't seem to care. No wonder he was so full of himself.

Slate was attractive. I'd give him that. He had the startling good looks that could stop traffic. But I didn't care about that. My heart wasn't moved by a handsome face and a chiseled body. It belonged to a guy in a hospital room and it always would. One day I'd tell Crawford about all the things that happened while he was asleep and we'd smile. Not because he had been in a coma, but because he woke up.

He was a fighter and he had a lot to fight for.

My phone vibrated in my bag and I knew the text messages had started up again. Last night I'd played basketball and eaten homemade strawberry cake with cream cheese icing while talking to Maddy about using the potty. Everyone had gotten a piece of me. They needed to give me a break today and just let me be.

I would be fine. When Crawford woke up.

CHAPTER FIVE

"AUNTIE VALE!" MADDY'S and Malyn's little voices rang down the halls of the hospital, drawing more than just my attention. Identical brown eyes like their mother's and long brown hair in pigtails swinging back and forth, they came running toward me with their arms open wide.

More than anything, I missed these two by being here all day long. I put my book down and stood up just in time to catch both of them. Little arms wrapped around me. Tears stung my eyes and I held them tightly.

"My favorite girls are here," I said, kissing them both on the forehead, then on their tiny noses.

"I figure if I can't get Maddy to potty at home I'd bring her to you," Dylan said, looking like the exasperated father of twin toddlers should look.

I felt real joy as I laughed with him. It was a fleeting feeling, but my big brother had brought it to me.

Pulling back enough so I could see their faces, I looked at Maddy. "You have to use the potty like a big girl even when I'm not there. Do you want Malyn to get to start big-girl school without you?" "Big-girl school" was preschool and they didn't start until the fall, but it was something both girls were excited about. I was supposed to go to college in the fall. Me and Crawford. Now that wasn't a sure thing anymore.

Maddy shrugged. "I want to stay with you."

What could I do with that? Worried, I glanced up at Dylan.

"She loves you and misses you," he said. "We all do."

Guilt. But I had to be here with Crawford when he opened his eyes. He'd want me here. I needed them all to understand that.

"I love and miss her, too. All of you. But you need to understand why I have to be here. What if it was Catherine?"

Dylan looked somber. "I get it. Doesn't mean I don't miss you and worry about you."

"I can do the spwits," Malyn said, pulling on my arm to get my attention back to her.

"You can?" I asked, sounding surprised even though I'd seen this trick about a thousand times already. Malyn loved to show it off. So I watched and then clapped like it was the best thing in the world.

"I can do this!" Maddy said, standing on her tiptoes and spinning in circles.

"Wow, that's amazing!" I told her, reaching out to steady her before she got dizzy and fell.

"Why don't we go show Aunt Vale how you use the big-girl potty," Dylan suggested. It must be time for a toilet break. "Malyn is in big-girl panties, but Maddy has Pull-Ups on," he informed me. Then he held out a diaper bag and sank down in the seat next to me. Daddy looked like he needed a break.

"Come on, you two." I led them down the hallway toward the restrooms.

We had just turned the corner when Maddy said, "Look, Aunt Vale. That boy's kissing that nurse."

I glanced over to see the nurse from this morning in a corner with Slate. His hand was on her bottom and she was pressed up against him like she needed him to breathe. A public display of "affection" in a hospital where people are ill and dying—seriously? Slate Allen was disgusting.

"Did she fix his boo-boo?" Malyn asked curiously.

I was sure he'd fixed a few boo-boos for her.

I turned their attention to the restroom door and got them focused on potty time. I even sang the song. Success with both of them. Maddy had kept her Pull-Ups dry, and after washing hands we headed back out to find an empty corner, thank God. No more make-out fest for the twins' curiosity.

My luck, however, quickly came to a halt when we turned the corner and saw Dylan talking with none other than the Nurse Romeo.

"Daddy, we went potty!" Maddy announced as she ran back toward the waiting room.

Malyn realized the guy with her dad was the same one she'd seen kissing the nurse. She slowed her step and slipped her little hand around my leg. She was the shyer of the two.

"You kissed that nurse! Did she fix your boo-boo?" Maddy got right to business.

The confusion on Dylan's face as he looked from Maddy to me almost made me laugh. Almost.

"Here's the bag. They're all good," I told him.

I felt Slate's gaze on me, and I just couldn't make myself be rude to him. So what if he'd been kissing a nurse. Why did I care? I didn't.

"Thanks," Dylan said, still looking confused.

"He kissed a nurse," Maddy announced again, pointing at Slate.

Slate glanced at Maddy, then at me like he wasn't sure if he'd done something wrong.

"So you know Slate, too?" I asked Dylan.

He shook his head. "Not until just now. He was looking for you. I introduced myself and he said he was a Kappa Sigma with Knox."

"And he kissed a nurse," Malyn added finally because no one was acknowledging Maddy's announcement.

"Yes, he did. We weren't supposed to see that, though, and it's rude to talk about it. So let's talk about something else," I finally said.

Maddy's shoulders dropped with disappointment.

"Can Aunt Vale come home with us?" Malyn asked, quickly moving along to a subject more interesting to her.

"Aunt Vale wants to stay with Crawford. Remember? She'll be at Nonna and Poppa's tonight for dessert. We will see her then," Dylan told his daughters.

I bent down to their eye level. "And you both can tell me about how big you both were and used the potty all day. No accidents."

"Can I stay the night with you if I do?" Maddy asked.

I was always exhausted in the evenings and Maddy kicked terribly all night. But I wasn't going to tell her no. "Yes, if your momma is okay with it."

"Oh, she will be," Dylan said with a pleased tone. He didn't get his wife alone much anymore.

"YAY!" they both cheered, and clapped their hands. I hugged them both and kissed their heads before standing up.

"I'll get these two home for their naps and we'll see you to-night," Dylan said. Then he looked at Slate. "Nice to meet you. Hope your uncle gets better."

Slate nodded, and I hugged my brother good-bye before the three of them left, him holding one little hand in each of his.

"Sorry about the kissing thing," Slate said, sounding sincere. "Didn't think about kids seeing it."

I bet he didn't think about much more than the bottom he was groping. I smiled, though, and shrugged. "Isn't like they haven't seen it before. Just never with a nurse. I hope she fixed you up," I teased, thinking about the boo-boo comment from Maddy.

He smirked. "Funny."

"That was the girls' main concern."

He laughed this time. "She came on to me."

I rolled my eyes. "Yeah, it looked like you were fighting her off."

"Never claimed to fight it off. Just that she started it."

I walked over to my seat and picked up my book. "Not my business, Slate Allen," I said, smiling to myself that I knew his last name.

"Sounds like someone is doing some research," he said, sounding pleased.

I laughed. "Not hardly. The nurse who attacked you came looking for you this morning and asked if Slate Allen had been in here. I found out completely by accident." I opened the book and then glanced up at him. "Looks like I gave good directions. You're welcome."

He studied me as if he was seeing me for the first time. It was a bit unsettling, so I turned back to my book.

"I'll see you tomorrow, Vale McKinley," he said, and I nodded but didn't look up.

With a soft chuckle he was gone.

One more hour before I could see Crawford.

CHAPTER SIX

MADDY WAS FINALLY asleep. Malyn had fallen asleep easily, but Maddy had been too excited. I covered her up and then eased myself out of the bed. I wanted some milk and another bite of the caramel pie Mom had in the fridge. Maddy had eaten most of my piece earlier.

I heard Knox and Mom talking in the kitchen, and I almost turned around and went right back into my room. Those two would want to talk about Crawford and my schedule. They loved me. I got it. But they needed to get that I was an adult. I was eighteen years old. I didn't need advice.

Taking a deep breath and preparing myself for a potential argument, I went down the eight stairs that it took to get to the first floor. Turning right, I walked straight into the kitchen. Knox was at the table with the entire pie plate and a fork. Not surprising.

"Save me some, pig," I said, going over to the drawer to get myself a fork.

"The rest is all yours," he said, sliding the plate over.

"You want milk, baby?" Momma asked.

"I can get it," I told her. She waited on my brothers, but I didn't like it. We should be waiting on Momma the way she did for us.

"Sit. I barely see you. Let me at least fix your milk."

I forced a smile and sat down with my pie. It was more than I'd eat, but I didn't tell Knox that. He'd eat the whole thing if I offered him more.

"Dylan said Slate stopped by again today," Knox said.

I nodded. "Yep." I decided telling him about the coffee was a bad idea.

"Be careful. You're a challenge to him. He's used to girls chasing him. He hasn't met a Vale yet."

I crammed a bite of pie in my mouth and glared at him. Was he seriously worried I was going to hook up with Slate Allen when all I did was sit outside my comatose boyfriend's hospital room waiting on him to open his eyes?

"I think it's good she has someone up there to talk to. I worry about her getting lonely," Momma said as she sat the milk down in front of me.

"Mom, he's a player. Sleeps with more women than Charlie Sheen."

Momma made a *tsk*ing sound. "Nonsense. No one has slept with more people than Charlie Sheen."

I laughed and Knox sighed. He wasn't amused. I thought Mom had made a funny.

"I'm serious. Not your kind of guy," he said, looking at me with a hard glare.

I was over this conversation. "Knox, I sit at a hospital all day every day waiting on the only guy I've ever loved and will ever love to open his eyes. That is my world. Do you honestly think I'm even entertaining the idea of Slate? What makes you think I would even notice him?"

"All females notice him."

I took another bite. I wasn't some sorority girl who wanted to be added to Slate Allen's bedpost notches. No thank you.

"I think you need to trust your sister," Momma said.

Knox grunted. "Just because you want her to have a life outside that hospital doesn't mean Slate Allen needs to be part of it."

I sat my fork down and stood back up. "I think I've had enough. I'm going to bed. Then in the morning I will go back to Crawford. I will always go back to Crawford."

"Finish your milk, honey," Momma said, sounding almost like she was pleading.

I didn't want to upset her, so I reached for my glass and started drinking.

"Wasn't trying to upset you." Knox sounded a bit guilty. "I'll come read to Crawford tomorrow. More college football stuff he needs to hear."

I finished my milk, then took the glass to the sink to wash it.

"I'm fine. And thank you. Crawford needs to hear us. This talk about Slate Allen is pointless, though."

Momma patted my back and kissed the top of my head. "I want you happy."

I couldn't be happy without Crawford. But I didn't tell her that. I just nodded.

"I know, Momma." I hugged her. "Good night and thanks for the pie."

"See you at lunch," Knox called out, and I waved without turning around, then headed back to my room. The security of silence. Where no one told me what they thought I should do.

Quietly I slipped back into my room to see my nieces sprawled out on my full-size bed. There wasn't any room left for me now. Smiling, I took the extra pillow and a blanket from the closet and curled up on the bean bag I still had on the floor from my childhood. The girls loved to play on it so I'd kept it.

Although I hadn't slept on it in years, I remembered nights I would fall asleep reading in it or talking on the phone to Crawford. That seemed like another lifetime ago. What I would give now to be able to just pick up the phone and call him. To hear his voice before I went to bed. To hear his laughter and know that tomorrow he would be there with me.

He had to wake up. I couldn't face this life without him. He was my safe place, my best friend. Tears stung my eyes and I let them fall. Feeling them run down my cheeks, the pain in my chest didn't ease, but it felt less lonely to cry.

Everything was different now. I was lost. Alone. I didn't know how to find myself. I needed Crawford. Knox worrying about me liking the wrong guy was ridiculous. I loved Crawford and I had my entire life. A pretty smile and incredible eyes weren't going to change that. I wasn't shallow.

Closing my eyes, I let myself remember life with Crawford.

Walking through the field, I saw the swing hanging from our favorite tree before we got to it. The thick ropes held a large flat piece of wood. I turned back to Crawford. "What's that?" I asked, pointing at the swing.

He grinned. "It looks to me like it's a swing, V."

"I know that . . . but where did it come from?"

He walked up and slipped his hand over mine. We were doing that a lot lately. Holding hands. "You said last week the only thing that could make this place better was a swing. So there's your swing."

My eyes grew wide as his words sank in. "You did that?"

"Well, my dad helped a little," he admitted.

31

That didn't matter. It had been his idea. He had built me a swing. "Can I try it?" I was unable to contain my excitement.

"You better. Or my feelings will be hurt."

I threw both arms around his neck while standing on my tiptoes to reach him. He grew an inch every day, it seemed. Soon I would need a ladder to reach him.

"Thank you," I said as his arms wrapped around me.

"Anything for you, V. Anything."

CHAPTER SEVEN

AS I WALKED down the hall toward the waiting room, my steps slowed when I saw Slate sitting there. He had a coffee in each hand. The same delicious coffee from yesterday. He was leaning back in a chair with his feet propped up on the seat across from him.

Why was he here this early? I'd been here an hour already when he'd arrived yesterday, and he had called that early. He turned his head in my direction as I got closer. Then a slow smile slid across his face that I would admit was movie star–worthy. He should look into that. Or modeling, maybe.

"Good morning," he said as if he'd been up for hours or had several cups of coffee. I'd had none and slept on a bean bag, then was awakened by Maddy before the sun was fully up.

"Why are you here?" I asked, not even attempting to sound polite. I was too tired for polite.

He held up the coffee. "Well, I thought that was obvious. Bringing a friend a cup of joe and seeing just how early she gets here every day." He glanced back at the clock on the wall. "Seven sharp. Impressive."

I was a challenge to him. That's what Knox had said. Maybe he was right.

The thing was, I didn't want to be a challenge. I had Crawford to worry about.

"Thanks for the coffee," I said, and took the one he was offering me. "Are you going to see your uncle now?"

He laughed. "No way. He'd kill me if I woke him up this early. He already bitches out the nurses for waking him up at eight to eat. Not a friendly guy."

And Slate made those nurses feel lots better, I was sure.

I put my bag down, then took a seat two over from him. There was no reason to sit too close. I wasn't into this challenge thing. Telling him so seemed like the best course of action.

"Knox mentioned that you like chasing girls and that I'm a challenge. Let's just be clear—I'm not. I love Crawford. I'll always love Crawford. No contest here. But I appreciate the coffee."

That didn't sound as sophisticated as I had hoped, but there it was.

When he didn't say anything right away, I glanced over at him, and he was taking a drink of his coffee while studying the wall like there was a piece of art on it rather than a clock.

"Do you know what I used to do at five every morning?" he asked.

Weird question and completely not on topic, but I went with it.

"What?"

He turned his head to me. "I used to get up and feed the chickens and collect their eggs, clean the horses' stalls—we had three—and then fill the water trough for the horses before feeding the dogs and going inside to get breakfast started. Uncle D drank too heavily every evening to get up and do much. So before school I handled that shit."

None of it even sounded believable and I didn't know why he was telling me this.

He stood up then and gave me a sincere smile. "Have a good day, Vale. I hope your boy opens his eyes."

Then he walked away.

I SAT FOR the next hour wondering what that conversation had meant and why Slate had told me such a strange story. He never reacted to what I said, and I started wondering if I'd imagined speaking to him. Once my coffee was gone and my legs were stiff from sitting, I got up and decided to walk around the hospital some. It always scared me to get too far away from Crawford, but I needed to stretch my legs. My sleeping arrangements last night had made me sore.

I took the elevator to the children's floor to see if they might need someone to read to the kids in the children's activity room. I needed something to do while I waited. I could at least be helpful.

A deep voice I recognized stopped me as I opened the door. I looked in the window behind the Dr. Seuss poster that covered most of the glass and saw Slate sitting in a large red chair with a book in his hands. Three little girls and two boys sat on the floor in front of him. Four of the five kids were bald. One little girl held a teddy bear tightly to her chest as she looked up at Slate with wide eyes.

He was reading. To the kids. And he was doing a good job

because he had their complete attention. I stood there and watched, letting the door close quietly. I didn't want him to see me, but I had to be sure that what I was seeing was for real. I didn't imagine Slate as a guy who would spend his morning reading to sick kids. But there he was, smiling and making different voices that made the kids laugh.

After a few moments, I stepped out and made my way back down to Crawford's floor. The image of Slate reading aloud wasn't going to leave me. He might be a player, but he was a nice guy. He had a heart. He was visiting me because I was alone, waiting for my boyfriend to wake up. Not once had he actually hit on me. I'd just assumed.

Over the next three days my coffee was waiting on me when I arrived, but there was no Slate. Not a sign of him. All day.

Finally the coffee and absent Slate got to me. When I went in to see Crawford at four, I sat my bag down and looked at him. "I've met this guy and he's messed with my head. I think I hurt his feelings and his uncle is very sick and he reads to the kids on the children's floor and I should have been more thoughtful. He didn't do anything but bring me coffee. He still brings me coffee. But he's never there. Doesn't stop by. I don't even see him in the halls making out with nurses. Yes, he makes out with the nurses in the halls. He is a player. According to Knox he's the worst kind of player. They're frat brothers. You know how frat boys are." Sighing, I sat down on the chair beside him and stared at the familiar face I missed so much. He was here, but he wasn't.

"I just need you to wake up. I'm losing it without you, Crawford."

There was no movement. No new brain activity. Nothing.

"Maybe he would have been a good friend. I need one of those. All of ours don't come around much. Seeing you upsets them and reminds them that life can change on a dime. I'm disappointed in them, but it's true. Braxton left for UA this week. He stopped in last week to say good-bye. But he felt awkward. They all do. I can see it."

Braxton had been Crawford's best guy friend most of our lives. Of all people, I was most surprised by Braxton's absence. In the beginning, everyone was here. Stopping by and bringing flowers, candy, balloons, and the like. Then after two weeks it slowed. Three weeks, not a soul. A month and they had all moved on to their summer thing. Vacations, packing for college, and moving.

It had gotten lonely. Slate was helping somewhat. He was a distraction. But I'd let Knox get to me and I'd been mean and run him off. Yet he still was kind enough to bring me coffee.

I should go check on his uncle. That was the nice thing to do. Show I care. I wondered if anyone other than Slate came to visit his uncle. Was he alone, too? Was that why he kept stopping by to visit me? He needed company that didn't want to crawl in his lap and lick his face? Possibly.

Stupid Knox. I shouldn't have listened to him.

"I think I'll go visit his uncle tomorrow. He has cancer and he's old. I bet he needs company. Besides, it's lonely in that waiting room."

Crawford didn't say anything. But then, he still hadn't opened his eyes.

"Ready for me to read chapter fifteen? I fell asleep before we got to it last night. Your mom had to wake me up. I'll try to stay awake longer tonight. But, of course, if you'd wake up I would stay awake forever. It's the silence that makes me sleepy. And possibly these machines."

I reached into my bag and pulled out a book and my bottle of water. After taking a long drink, I got comfortable and opened the book to chapter fifteen. It was time the search party got serious. "Hope this ends good. I should have Googled it before I started reading it," I told him.

CHAPTER EIGHT

KNOX WAS SITTING in the kitchen with a glass of milk and some brownies when I walked in the house. He always seemed to be eating lately. It was a miracle he stayed so slim.

"Where's everyone?" I asked, setting my bag on the bar and going to the fridge for leftovers. I was starving. It had been a while since lunch.

"Mom is at Dylan's watching the girls while they go on a date. Dad's over at Rob's watching baseball. I'm staying here to check on the baby"—he pointed his fork at me as if I didn't know what baby he was talking about—"to ease everyone's mind. It's Friday night. You're young and should be out enjoying life."

"Not in the mood for this," I told him as I spooned some mac and cheese onto a paper plate.

"You seen any more of Slate?"

That annoyed me. I set the spoon down. "No, as a matter of fact. Not in three days. Not since I told him I wasn't a challenge and not to chase me."

Knox's eyes went wide, then he started laughing. I was very close to tossing the spoon at his head. Or better yet, the whole bowl of mac and cheese. But Mom would kill me. She didn't like to waste food. Although if I did toss it, I could let Bruno inside so he could lick it clean. He'd love that. Feeding our chocolate lab wouldn't be considered wasting food. Technically.

"You told him not to chase you?" Knox barked with laughter again.

"I'm seriously close to making you wear this mac and cheese," I warned him.

He shook his head and tried to stop laughing. He didn't do a very good job. I turned my back on him and put my plate in the microwave. He had me all worked up over Slate and now he was laughing about my handling it. I didn't understand brothers at all.

"I'm sorry," he said through his laughter. "I am just picturing Slate's face when you told him. That is definitely something he's never heard before."

I glared at the microwave. "Well, it worked. He's not come back around."

Knox's laughter faded. "You don't seem happy about that."

I wasn't. I was afraid I'd hurt his feelings, and dang it, I was lonely during the day. Slate's visits had been nice.

"I think I hurt his feelings."

My mac and cheese was done, and I took it out then walked over to the table.

"You didn't hurt his feelings. He's tougher than that. If anything, you confirmed what he already knew. You weren't his normal. You're too good for that. Glad he got the point. We're brothers and all, but blood is thicker than Kappa Sigma. Just don't tell them I said that."

"I think I should go visit his uncle—I don't want to be rude. And Slate brings me good coffee every morning. He just leaves it for me before I get there. That's nice of him."

Knox grunted. "Yeah, fucking thoughtful."

I rolled my eyes and ate my meal. I was too tired for this tonight.

"Vale, what if he never wakes up? Are you going to spend your life going to that hospital every day? I mean, I love Crawford, too. He was like a brother to me. I hate that this has happened, but it's been a month. You've got to start learning to live without him."

This wasn't the first time I'd heard this. Not from Knox or the rest of our family. I was tired of it. They didn't understand.

"I love him."

"And he loved you. He wouldn't want this for you."

That I believed. I knew Crawford would want me living outside of those hospital walls. But how could he expect that when he was still in there? I couldn't just leave him. He needed me.

"It's all I can do to make it through each day. I have to be there."

Knox sighed and stood up. "I hope he opens his eyes soon."

That was something we could agree on.

"Me too."

"There's the chance he won't. If he doesn't, you're going to have to eventually learn to live. I can't sit back and watch your life tick by while you sit in that hospital. None of us can. Start preparing yourself for the worst, sis. It could happen."

I hated hearing that. I knew it was true, but I hated hearing it. Crawford was stronger than that. He'd open his eyes. He would come back to me. To our life. He had to.

"You're still enrolled at Bington for the fall semester. I'd like for you to go back with me when it's time. You're going to like it there and it's close. Just an hour drive. You don't have to live on campus, but your dorm is paid and I think you'd like it. Be a good scenery change."

I couldn't think about that now. I knew I had to make a decision soon about college, but not now. Not yet. I needed more time. Crawford needed more time.

"I can't deal with this right now."

"You've been saying that for a month, Vale. It's almost July. August will be here before you know it, and you'll have to make a decision."

I knew all this. Closing my eyes tightly, I took a deep breath to calm down. I wanted to scream at him to stop. I knew he meant well, but he didn't understand. Bington had been my and Crawford's plan. How did I go there without him?

"It's only been a month," I said, knowing it had been five weeks now. Each day that passed and he didn't open his eyes, my fear that he wouldn't grew.

"I know," Knox said softly, then walked over and squeezed my shoulder gently. "I just love you and want the best for you."

"I need more time."

"Okay," he said, then finally left me to myself. I knew this argument was coming again from my parents. I expected it. They had paid for my tuition and dorm already. I couldn't expect them to not want answers or a decision. I had to give that to them. But how?

Should I postpone college for Crawford? Was that a mistake? Could I leave him?

No. I couldn't. He wouldn't leave me. I knew that. He'd need me here when he opened his eyes. I couldn't allow myself to plan a future that didn't have him in it. That was letting him down. He'd never let me down. Not once.

I finished my meal, then cleaned up my mess before heading up to take a shower. Tomorrow might be the same as it had been for the past five weeks. But I still hoped for the miracle we were all waiting on.

CHAPTER NINE

FOR THE FIRST time since the accident, I overslept. My alarm hadn't gone off, which was odd because I was sure I had set it last night. I always set it. The clock said it was almost ten. How had I slept so late?

Getting dressed in a crazed hurry, I skipped breakfast and ran straight out the door. Mom had called out after me that she had made me a bagel to go but I didn't have time to respond. I was supposed to be at the hospital. Why hadn't Knox woken me up? He was going to read to Crawford at ten today. He should have realized I hadn't left yet.

As I gripped the steering wheel, it dawned on me that he did know I was still sleeping and he'd left me to sleep. I knew he meant well, but I knew what was best for me. I didn't need his or my mother's interference. I wouldn't be surprised if he had turned off my alarm himself.

They all needed to let me deal with this the way I wanted to. The way I needed to. They didn't understand. Crawford would want me there. When his eyes opened, he would want to see me. Leaving me at home like that was just wrong. I'd tell Knox that when I saw him.

I parked quickly and ran the rest of the way. I knew Crawford's mother would have stepped out to get some fresh air while Knox was reading to Crawford, so I went straight to his room. I wouldn't argue with him in front of Crawford, but I'd glare at him and let him know how angry I was.

Jerking open the door to Crawford's room, I stepped inside and then immediately froze. That wasn't Knox's voice or the back of Knox's head. That was Slate. Reading. To Crawford.

Stepping closer, I listened to his deep drawl and tried to figure out why he was in Crawford's room reading to him. Reading to the kids was one thing, but this was something altogether different.

"Looks like the SEC is set up this year. Football should be interesting. Even your Vols look good. It's been a while since that happened."

He was holding a sports magazine and talking to Crawford. Like they were friends. Like he cared about Crawford.

I took another step, and he turned this time to look at me. Then that slow, lazy grin spread across his face. "Well, it looks like your girl got here. Looking pretty as ever."

I wouldn't blush at his compliment. "Why are you here?" I blurted out, then wished I hadn't. It sounded rude. "What I mean is, where is Knox?"

Slate leaned back and smirked. "Knox got a call and needed to run somewhere. Sounded important. He'd seen me in the hall earlier, so he came and asked me if I'd finish up reading."

He had something important to run off and do? And left Crawford with a stranger to read to him? Knox wasn't looking good today.

"Well, thank you. If he'd woken me up this morning before he left, I could have read to him. Not sure what his deal is today."

Slate shrugged. "I didn't mind. Besides, he mentioned you

were sleeping late and that was rare. He worries about you, is all. A brother thing, I guess."

I didn't want to be worried about. I was fine! I was walking around and breathing on my own, so I was absolutely fine! Crawford was not.

"He needs to back off. They all do," I muttered.

Slate closed the magazine. "Good luck with that. Family can be a bitch even when they're trying to do what's best." Then he stood up. "I'll leave you with him. I have a poker game to go finish with my uncle."

He'd left his uncle to come read to Crawford. He might be a playboy, but he was also a good guy. The world was bigger than the little protective bubble I'd been raised in. Things like sex didn't define people. They could be good and not be Sunday School material.

"Thank you for reading to him."

Slate nodded. "My pleasure. Anytime you need help, just give me a shout."

I watched as he walked out of the room. He really did have his own special swagger. It was hard not to watch. The bad-boy persona fit him well. But now I had been given a peek into his heart. And apparently it was pretty big. Not self-centered like I had thought. His uncle, the kids, now Crawford.

I owed him an apology. I just wasn't sure how to give him one. He might not even know I had judged him so unfairly. I turned my attention back to Crawford. He'd like Slate. I was positive Slate would entertain him. Crawford wasn't one to judge people.

"You look good this morning. Enjoy your update on the SEC football season?" I asked, knowing I wouldn't get an answer. I had the book I was reading to him, but for now I just wanted to talk.

"It'll be time to go to college soon. My parents have already started in on me. Especially Mom. I just can't imagine going without you." I wanted to beg him to open his eyes, but I didn't. I had done that enough.

"Staying here is all I can think of right now. Being next to you. Seeing you. It's what I need to cope. I miss you, Crawford. I miss you so much."

The door opened behind me and Crawford's mother walked in. She frowned upon seeing me and that hurt. Having me around bothered her, and all I could figure was that it was because I'd walked away from that crash and he didn't.

"Where's Knox?" she asked.

"He had to leave early. I stepped in to take over until you returned."

I didn't tell her about Slate in case she wouldn't be okay with that. He'd done a good thing, although Knox had better have a good excuse as to why he'd left early.

"Fine. I'll take over now. See you at four," she said.

I looked at Crawford. I wanted to say more, but I was also afraid to. I stood and tried to remember a time when seeing me didn't make Juliet frown. Back when Crawford was full of life. Back when we had a future planned.

"I spoke with your mother. You need to go to college, Vale. We don't know when Crawford will wake up and you sitting here every day isn't going to make it happen faster. He would want you to go to college. Live the life y'all had planned and just come visit."

I didn't expect to hear this from her. I assumed she wouldn't forgive me if I left for college without him. She was falling apart daily and he was her world. My leaving would be a betrayal. Didn't she see it that way?

"I don't think I can leave him."

She straightened her shoulders that were now so often slumped over. "I'm not your mother and I can't force you to do anything. But when Crawford wakes up, he will not want to know you wasted your life up here waiting on him. He'll blame himself for it. I don't want him to awaken to anything that will upset him. Think about him instead of yourself for a change. You always did make him do what you wanted. He never got to make his own decisions if he wanted to keep you happy."

That stung. Deep. I had no words for that, so I managed a weak nod and left the room. Remembering the problems in our life wasn't easy. Because although I loved Crawford, things hadn't been easy before. His mother adored him, and because of that, she wasn't always happy with me. I never did seem to treat him the way she thought I should. Although I tried so hard to make him happy.

Was I thinking of only myself by staying here?

CHAPTER TEN

NO ONE CONFESSED to turning off my alarm. Knox seemed to be the obvious culprit, so I hid my clock under my pillow to make sure it wouldn't happen again. As for his leaving Crawford early, Dylan had gotten a flat tire on the interstate with both the twins in the car with him. He'd needed backup so he could get the tire changed. So Knox hadn't been in as much trouble as I first assumed.

However, when Knox came walking up with Slate at nine thirty, I was a little confused. He was supposed to be reading to Crawford today at ten. He'd told me last night he was making up for leaving yesterday. So why did he have Slate here again?

Slate handed me a cup of coffee. "Morning, Vale."

"Good morning, and thank you," I replied, still trying to figure out if Slate had just bumped into Knox or if they were here together.

"Figured if I was coming in early for another reading session, you could use some good coffee."

Another reading session? I jerked my gaze to Knox. I didn't need to say anything for him to understand my thoughts. He put both his hands in the air as if to hold me off him. "Don't look at me.

Juliet called me last night and said the doctors had said Crawford's brain waves had more action yesterday in the hour of ten to eleven than normal. Whatever had happened needed to repeat itself." He nodded toward Slate. "Slate happened—so here he is to read again and see if it works."

Slate? Crawford's brain waves were picking up for Slate? Seriously?

"What did you read him again?" I asked, trying not to be jealous.

He held up the magazine in his hand. "College football."

Knox read him that all the time. It made no sense.

"I don't understand," I said, finding myself trying not to be angry with Slate. It wasn't like he did something wrong.

"I told Juliet it was Slate reading during that time and why, and she asked if he'd come back. So I went to him thinking I'd need to bribe him—but being the great guy he is, he agreed to return. So let's see if this works a second time."

I wanted to go in there, too. But I knew Juliet wouldn't let me. She'd want it to happen just like yesterday.

I sank down into a chair and took a drink of my coffee. It should be me who Crawford responded to. It should be my voice that brought him out of the coma. Because he wanted to be with me.

"I'm going to introduce Slate to Juliet. I'll be back out in a minute and we can go to the cafeteria and grab some food—no arguments," Knox told me.

I would argue, but I didn't have it in me. I was too hurt. Silly to be hurt over this, but I was. Maybe Crawford didn't want me to stay. Maybe he did want me to go to college. Was I being selfish? Juliet had accused me several times over the years of being selfish. Not thinking of Crawford's needs. When in reality I was going to the college Crawford wanted to go to. I always had gone to the places he wanted and eaten at the restaurants he wanted. I even wore the clothes he liked. I couldn't figure out how I was being selfish. I had been trying for years to not be.

The thought of going to college without Crawford was terrifying. But if he would want that, then how was I supposed to not go? I wanted him to wake up happy. Glad to be alive. Not full of regrets.

Knox was walking back to me. "Figures it would be Slate that entertained Crawford the most. The guy is hilarious. I'll give him that."

I managed a smile that I didn't feel and stood back up. For once I needed out of this waiting room. I needed space to think. Doing what was best for Crawford was my only concern.

"Why don't you ever think about what you want, Vale?" My mother's voice rang in my head. She had asked me that many times over the years. She never did understand that I did think about myself. I just wanted what Crawford wanted. Why wasn't that okay?

"How do I leave him? How do I go to college without him?" I asked Knox as we began walking toward the elevators.

"A day at a time. He would want you to."

I'd always done what Crawford wanted. But he had never wanted something that would hurt so much.

"It scares me," I admitted.

Knox put his arm around my shoulder. "I'll be there. You won't be alone. When you get scared, all you have to do is call me. Just a few buildings away. It's time you did something other than sit here."

He didn't get it. None of them got it.

"Juliet said Crawford would want me to go. That I was being selfish to stay."

Knox sighed. "Nothing about you is selfish. Never has been and never will be. You're the most selfless person I know. But she's right about Crawford. He'd never want you to stay here like this."

I wanted to curl into a ball and cry. For all we had lost. For the future I'd never planned alone. For the past that would never be the same.

"Crawford's a good guy. He loves you. He always has. But he wasn't perfect, Vale. He expected you to do what he wanted. That bugged the hell out of me. It's time you make some decisions on your own. Make a life that *you* are in charge of."

As much as I didn't like hearing that, I realized my brother was right. I let Crawford make decisions for me. I wanted to make him happy, and I was so worried about being selfish. Had I missed that all along? Did I lose myself somewhere along the way?

"It's like finding myself again." That was something I would only admit to Knox.

"It is way past time," he replied with a squeeze of my shoulders.

Being who I wanted to be was confusing. Because I wasn't sure anymore.

I stood there in that elevator beside my brother and let the past few years play over in my head. How I had slowly changed. How I had let Crawford begin to mold me. I don't think he meant to. I just allowed it.

But it was me he fell in love with in the first place. Not the girl I'd turned into. When he woke up I'd be ready, and I realized that that would make him the happiest.

CHAPTER ELEVEN

SLATE READING TO Crawford had once again made his brain activity pick up. When Knox called to tell Slate, he agreed to come read to him while he was still in town with his uncle. No one had an explanation for why Slate's reading did more than anyone else's. But Juliet was thrilled. It had given her some hope.

Tonight when she'd left me with Crawford, she had a smile. A small one, but still a smile. I hadn't seen one of those from her in a long time.

I was tempted to read him the SEC magazine myself and see what happened. But I didn't. Tonight I needed to talk to him. Tell him what I was thinking. Before I told my parents and started to prepare to go to college next month, I had to tell Crawford.

I set down my bag and walked over and touched his hand. It was cold in his room, so his hand was always cold. I wanted to warm it up. I hated to think he might be cold.

"Everyone says you would want me to go to college. Your mom, Knox, my parents. They all think it's what's best. When you wake up, they say you'll be happy I lived, that I went on like we planned. As much as it scares me and as much as I want to be here with you, I think it's time I made my own decisions. I lost myself somewhere along the way. Maybe you noticed and just didn't know how to tell me. Maybe you didn't. I don't know anymore." I paused and let out a sigh. Telling him all this was difficult. Even if he didn't hear me or remember any of it.

"I'm going to tell my parents tonight. I'll go next month. I'll take the classes I planned and come home on the weekends to visit you. I can read you whatever novel they have me reading in class. I can tell you all about it. Or you can wake up and come, too. That would be what I really want."

I wasn't supposed to pressure him. Juliet was afraid it would upset him. But he needed to know I'd want him with me more than anything else. "Until you're ready to join me, I'll figure things out. Find the best coffee shops, pizza places, and study spots. When you get there, I can update you on all of it.

"I'm not leaving you. Don't think that. I will come back every chance I get. I'll tell you about everything. When you open your eyes, you'll know I did this for you. Not me. Because I just want to stay here."

I think. *Was that what I wanted? Really?* Because I was lonely here. Lost. Out of place. More things I couldn't tell him. In the past when I told him I could never make his mother happy, he disagreed and said she loved me. He saw things differently than I did.

"Tomorrow I'm not going to sit in the waiting room all day. I'm going to shop for school. Spend some time with my mom. The twins, too. I'll be here at four, though. I just need to slowly move away from being here all the time. So I'll be prepared when it's time for me to leave. You understand that, right?"

He wouldn't answer. I didn't expect him to. But I asked him anyway.

WHEN I WALKED into the house at eight thirty I could smell the meat loaf that mom had cooked for dinner. She wrapped it in bacon, and that distinct smell hung around for hours. There was also the sweet smell of apples in the air. I was ready to eat for a change. Ready to do something for me.

"You're home just in time," Mom said, peeking her head out the kitchen door. "I just pulled the apple tarts out of the oven. They're nice and warm. You can eat dessert first. Just don't tell Knox."

"He's obviously not here, or he'd be standing at that stove waiting for you to pull them out of the oven."

Mom chuckled. "You're right about that. He's gone to meet up with some friends in town. Or something like that."

Immediately I wondered if Slate was one of them. Was he meeting his frat brothers? What were they doing? None of it was my business, and I didn't know why I cared.

"I'm going to college next month," I said, watching Mom freeze, then put down the plate she'd been holding. She stood there a moment, then squealed before throwing her arms around me. I hugged her back.

"Oh, baby, I'm so glad. Lord knows I've wanted to hear those words for weeks. You won't regret this." She kept hugging me and I could hear the emotion clogging her throat. I'd worried her. I felt guilty about it. I hated that I hadn't thought about her needs. Was that what Juliet meant by me being selfish?

"I needed time. To decide what was best for me." I didn't add what was best for Crawford. Because I had to stop that. I was doing all I could for him. This wasn't about making him happy. A relationship was about us both being happy.

"I know," Mom said, sniffling, then laughing at herself as she released me to wipe at her tears. "These are happy tears. Can't seem to help it. This is such a relief. Go ahead and eat all the tarts. Forget about dinner if you want."

This time I laughed. "I actually want the meat loaf, Mom."

"Then help yourself!" she said, clapping her hands and laughing some more with tear-filled eyes. "Just live again, Vale."

Living had seemed wrong. Since the moment of the accident, it had seemed like I was doing something terrible if I lived. Crawford wasn't getting to live, so why should I? That wasn't the way to look at this, though. It had been selfish to think that way. Crawford loved me. My self-punishment wouldn't please him. He'd hate it.

"Let me fix you a plate. I even made the mashed potatoes just the way you like them. No skins and creamy."

I sat down and let Mom fuss over me. It made her feel good and it was time she got to feel good again. She'd been suffering in her own way and that was my fault. I wasn't doing that to her anymore.

"Juliet's gonna be happy to hear this. She was just telling me the other day how she wants you to go. How Crawford would want you to go."

I nodded. I already knew this. I just had to finally accept it.

CHAPTER TWELVE

TRUE TO HIS word, Slate came up to the hospital to read to Crawford several times a week. After my shopping day with Mom, I changed my schedule up some. I had breakfast at home, then went to the hospital to check on things. I left and spent time with Malyn and Maddy, or went home to pack things and visit with my mom. Then I would drive back at four when it was my time with Crawford.

It wasn't easy at first, but the new routine made me feel less guilty about neglecting those who loved me, and I felt like I'd gotten more accomplished every night when I lay down to sleep. Something Crawford would be happy about. Knowing that I was happy, too. This was what I needed, even if I hadn't thought so to begin with.

It was the second week into the new schedule when I arrived just as Slate was leaving. I wouldn't get to actually go in the room with Crawford. I'd arrive early to talk to Juliet or the nurses. It helped to stop by and get an update.

"Hey," I said to Slate as I stepped off the elevator he had been waiting to get on. I felt like I should have a coffee for him.

"Hey yourself. He's doing good today. Doctor says he's

seeing more activity out of him daily. Heard you were planning on coming our way next month. Glad to hear it."

I nodded. "Yeah. I've been getting things ready to move in to my dorm."

He smiled. "Dorm life. Gotta love it." He paused, then nodded to the elevator that had now shut without him in it. "Want to go get a coffee with me?"

A couple weeks ago I would have said no. But now I had to think about it. A cup of coffee with a guy who was helping out my boyfriend didn't sound like a bad idea. I owed it to him.

"Sure. I could use a cup."

He grinned and, honestly, that smile was something else. I felt guilty for even thinking it, so I turned my attention to the elevator and pressed the down button again.

"I've got to be back here in two hours for a game of poker with my uncle. But the coffee shop where I've been getting the good stuff is about a mile from here."

"That's fine with me. I have time. I don't get in to see Crawford until four."

Slate was quiet a moment while we took the elevator down to the first floor. When we stepped off, he glanced at me. "So, you haven't been here as much. Not that it's my business. I was just curious as to the change."

I was sure Knox had told him something, if not explained it all. Or maybe he hadn't asked. I pulled my purse up higher on my shoulder, which was a nervous habit, and kept walking in step beside him.

"I was being selfish. My family missed me and was worried about me. Crawford doesn't know when I'm there, except hopefully when I read to him and talk to him every afternoon. I want to believe he can hear me then. But the rest of the time my family needs to see me live. It's hard. I feel like I shouldn't be living while he's in there, but I can't keep doing that to them. It's wrong."

Slate let out a sigh. "Yeah, well, I never put the word *selfish* and you in the same category. But it's nice of you to think of them."

I shrugged. "It's been hard on them. All of this. Me withdrawing. They worry about me. I had to start thinking about what Crawford would want when he wakes up. And if he sees I put life on hold for him, he'll be upset. He will feel like it's his fault. Again, I was selfish. I had to adjust my guilt and realize I needed to try to live normally."

The fact I was telling Slate all this was surprising. We hardly knew each other, but here I was opening up to him like he was a close friend. Why? I had no idea.

"I'll agree that if Crawford loves you as much as you obviously love him, he'd want you to live life. It's what you would want for him if the roles were reversed."

I didn't hesitate. "Absolutely."

"My car is on the third level," he said as we stepped outside.

"Mine is right over there. Aren't you coming back?" I asked, glancing over at him for the first time during our little conversation.

He nodded.

"Then just ride with me."

A small smile touched his lips. "You know, Vale, I think you may be my first female friend. It's kind of nice."

I'd had many male friends. They were also Crawford's friends and that made them mine as well. I could see why Slate didn't have female friends. They all wanted more from him.

"First time for everything. Besides, I'll need a friend once I get to school."

He chuckled. "Yeah, well, convincing anyone that you're just my friend will be comical. No one will believe it."

I unlocked my car door before we approached, then smiled over at him. "It may help your reputation."

"Or destroy it," he added.

I could tell by the look on his face he was teasing, although I knew there was a side to Slate I doubted many saw. The guy who read to kids at the hospital, or read to someone who was comatose who he'd never met. That guy was very different from the one I saw making out with a nurse in the hallway. He had many different parts to him . . . I wondered why he chose not to showcase the good stuff as much as he did the rest.

"Are you going to scare the shit out of me, or are you a good driver?" he asked as we climbed into my car.

"I'm an excellent driver," I assured him. Because I was. Especially after the wreck. I'd become an even more cautious driver.

He sank down into my leather passenger seat and leaned back. "All right. I'm going to trust you."

Smiling, I turned on the car and pulled out of the parking space. This was nice. Having someone to talk to again who wasn't a family member hovering and worrying over me.

"What happens when he wakes up?" Slate asked me.

That was an odd question. And I wasn't sure. Did I come home? Would he want me to? I frowned and focused on the road, but I didn't respond.

CHAPTER THIRTEEN

MY PARENTS' CAR was packed full of all my dorm decorations and needs. My Honda Civic was full of clothing and shoes. Parking for my building wasn't too far of a walk from the main entrance to the dorm. Dad had pulled up to unload and Knox was helping him. Knox had packed his truck with the few things he would need when he moved into his frat house this year. Only juniors and seniors got to live in the frat houses.

I thought about Slate then. Wondered if he'd be living in the frat house, too. If I'd see him any. After coffee that day, he'd gotten my phone number and said we'd text and have coffee. But he still hadn't texted or called.

"Your room's on the third floor. Turn left when you get off the elevator—it's the last room on the right. Door's open and your roommate is already in there." Knox paused and grinned. "I might have to stop by and visit my little sister often."

Great—my brother liked my roommate. That should be fun.

Dad laughed and took another box out of the car and headed for the entrance. Mom came up beside me as I stood there and looked up at the tall seven-story building that would be my home this year. It was intimidating, and I wasn't sure I was ready for this.

"I know it doesn't seem like it right now, but you're about to have some of the best days of your life."

I knew my mother meant it. She even believed it. But how was that possible without Crawford? I couldn't respond to that. I knew she wanted me to agree or even say I hoped so.

"He should be here" was what I said instead. "Unloading his own stuff and then coming to my room to help me unpack before going out together to explore." That was how this should have been.

"But he's not," she said. "Life tosses you things you're not expecting. This won't be the only big hurdle in your life. What you have to learn is that you're strong enough to live anyway. Despite missing him, you can find happiness again."

I reached down and picked up the suitcase I'd brought from my car. "I'm going to do my best," I told her.

"I know you will."

Being only an hour away from home helped. Knowing I could run home when I needed my room and a place to hide gave me a sense of peace about all this. Until Crawford opened his eyes and this became the life we had planned. Not the one I was trying to build alone.

The inside of the building was exactly as I imagined it. Sofas with coffee tables and candles lit in the middle of them made small gatherings all over the main lobby. There was an unlit fireplace as the centerpiece against the far wall. We headed for the elevators that already had a line forming and I felt more comfortable seeing other girls who were also new with their parents. Suitcases and boxes were everywhere. Girls who were returning were easy to spot, because as they were reunited with friends they hugged.

It took three elevator loads before it was our turn to get on.

"Like this every year. I said I wouldn't come until Sunday this time, but I cracked and came today like everyone else. So ready to get away from my hometown. You know?" a redhead with attractive freckles on her nose and short curly hair said as she smiled at me.

I didn't know about wanting to leave home. Leaving had been hard, but I didn't say that. I just returned her smile and nodded. "I wasn't prepared for how busy it is. Guess I should have thought about it."

The girl nodded and sighed. "As the day progresses it gets more insane. Be glad you're early." She stuck her travel mug under her left arm, then held out her right hand. "Mae," she said. "I'm a sophomore this year. I'm guessing you're a freshman."

I shook her hand. "Yeah. I'm Vale. Nice to meet you."

Her large expressive eyes seemed to twinkle. "Oh, I love that name. I have a thing for unique names. I even have a journal full of them. I'm adding Vale to it." She laughed. "I swear I'm not a stalker weirdo. I was just born with a name like Mae Rose, and that's so boring it's sad. I refuse to saddle my kids with the same. I've been saving names I like since I was seven."

As odd as that sounded, I liked this girl. She was very real. And chatty. I wouldn't have to talk much with her. She'd do all the talking.

"Makes complete sense," I told her, then remembered my mother was standing beside me. "This is my mom," I told her.

Again she stuck her coffee under her arm since she was holding hang-up clothes and shook my mother's hand. "Nice to meet you. Vale is going to love it here."

"I believe so, too," Mom agreed.

The elevator opened at the third floor and Knox and Dad were there waiting.

"Took y'all long enough," Knox said.

"Oh, stop grumbling. You've been flirting. You're just fine," Dad said, rolling his eyes.

"Is that your brother?" Mae asked, her eyes going wide.

"Yeah, and some days I'm glad."

She smiled and made a nervous giggle. Knox winked at her. Jesus. What kind of year was I in for?

CHAPTER FOURTEEN

I WAS ROOMING with Barbie. I'm not exaggerating here. Not even a little. Everly Adali Lane was five feet nine inches tall with blond hair that fell down her back, and blue eyes that were as dark as the ocean, unlike my light blue. Her lips looked super full, almost as if she'd had a little augmentation to them, and she had a tiny waist.

She was also a princess. I grew up with brothers. I didn't always put on makeup and I liked my Converse just fine. From the way this girl was dressed to move in to our dorm today, you would think she was headed out on a hot date. This was going to be interesting.

"Oh, it's just white," she said as my mother finished making up my twin-size bed with the comforter I had picked out for it. The comforter set was in fact white and had a simple ruffle on the ends. I liked it.

"What, my comforter?" I asked, looking toward the bed she was staring at.

"Yes . . ." she said slowly, as if she still couldn't comprehend the fact that it was white. Why was this so shocking?

"Do you have some colorful pillows, at least?" she asked.

"Uh, no." I was still watching her. Almost afraid she was going to have a head explosion or something.

She reached into a large basket by her bed and pulled out a furry cotton-candy-pink pillow and tossed it onto my bed. "There. Use that."

My mother glanced at me with her eyebrows darted up like she, too, had no idea what to think about this girl.

"Okay, thanks," I said, not sure if I was thankful or not. The furry pillow was kind of silly-looking.

"I also have some artwork that we can put around the room so it all flows better. You're not planning on hanging posters, are you? Because I can't live with posters."

Everly Adali was in luck. I hadn't even thought of posters. I had in fact bought a mirror, but it was oval and in a white wooden frame. I was almost afraid to get it out. "No posters," I assured her.

"Best news I've heard all day," she said brightly, then began to spray what looked like perfume on my bed and then hers. "It's lavender and vanilla. I got it in the Cotswolds while traveling around England this summer. You'll sleep better. Do you snore?"

"Like a sawmill," my dad said as he walked into the room with the last box. Knox had already headed to the frat house and promised to check in later. This would be where I did my good-byes to my parents, then was left with Everly.

"Thanks, Dad," I said, taking the box and placing it by the closet.

"I guess it's yours from here," Mom said, and hugged me. "Enjoy life again," she whispered in my ear.

"I'm going to try," I promised.

Dad hugged me. "If you get homesick, I'll fill you up with gas when you get home."

Smiling, I squeezed him. "Noted."

"Love you, baby girl," he whispered.

"Love you, too," I said.

They each kissed my cheek, then they left me there. With all my boxes and my new life.

"So you snore," Everly said, when they finally left the room.

I had forgotten that question. I could tell her I was a terrible snorer and let her worry about it all day. Or I could try to be friends with this girl.

"Not at all," I assured her.

She made a dramatic sigh of relief. "Ah, great. Okay. Well, I've got an afternoon coffee hook-up from a hottie I've been after since last year."

I wasn't surprised. Her skirt barely covered her bottom and her stomach was flashing from the crop top she was wearing.

"Okay. Enjoy yourself."

She beamed at me. "I will."

ONCE EVERLY WAS gone, I sank down onto my bed and let out a sigh. I had seven boxes left to unpack. The new surroundings were nice. My room at home had started being less of a place of solitude and more of a reminder of all that had changed.

Everything was fresh here. Different.

I stood up and went to the first box. Right on top was the photo of Crawford and me at prom. It was in a silver frame that I'd shopped for just a week before the accident. I sat the picture on the nightstand and the familiar stabbing in my chest returned.

I missed him. I missed him so much.

That smile wasn't one I'd seen in—it seemed forever now. Just seeing him smile used to make me feel at ease. I would do anything to get him to smile. But I realized that often I did whatever he asked, and didn't think about what *I* actually wanted. Had I really lost myself over the years in trying to please him? Had he noticed?

I looked around the room again. One thing was for sure—I was finding me now. When he did wake up, I wouldn't be the same girl. I'd be the one he fell in love with in the beginning.

Mom was right. This was my new start. I had to be strong and learn to live my life. It didn't mean I'd forget the life I'd had with Crawford. That was part of who I was. It would always be there.

When he woke up, so much would change yet again. I shook my head. I couldn't think about that right now. I would finish unpacking and find food. Maybe go to the gathering hall downstairs and see if Mae was around. I liked her better than my roommate anyway. And with that thought, I glanced back at the pink furry pillow on my bed and rolled my eyes.

My clothes barely fit in my closet. Mom had gone overboard. I had more pairs of shoes than one actually needed and my matching teal-blue towels had *V* monogrammed on them simply because my mother had a monogramming machine and she thought I wouldn't lose them this way.

The bathroom that I was to share with Everly was packed with all her stuff, so I was thankful I had baskets to put my things in and neatly stack against the wall by my closet. Once everything had a place, I broke down the boxes and went to read my welcome letter again because I knew it had said something about where to take the recyclables. Especially the boxes, since there would be plenty this weekend.

After reading over the directions twice and memorizing them, I picked up my stack and headed for the door. The line for the elevator was worse, so I decided to take the stairs since I was just on the third floor. I had to go to the bottom, then out the back entrance, take a left, and find the first blue Dumpster.

I dropped a few boxes off the top three times before I got to the bottom of the stairs. The elevator may have been easier. But I was here now, so I headed out the door and toward the Dumpster. My forehead had broken out into a sweat and my arms were burning.

"Here, let me help," a guy I couldn't see because of the stack of boxes said, and then they were gone. I had never been so thankful. "Got them," he said, as if I hadn't already realized that.

"Thanks," I told him, sounding way too winded and out of shape.

"No problem. I just hauled my sister's down here."

He was tall and a ginger. He was the attractive kind of ginger, though. Very Prince Harry. His muscles were impressive and on display with his T-shirt. I didn't stare, though. That would be rude.

"That's nice of you. My brother didn't hang around that long, but in his defense he had to go unpack himself. "

"I don't know how nice it was of me. My parents made me swear I'd help Mae until she was finished. And if I bailed she'd have called our dad. So . . ." He shrugged, then grinned.

"Mae, as in the girl who writes unique names in a journal?" I asked, thinking it would make sense for them to be siblings. Both redheads with friendly personalities.

"That would be Mae, her and that stupid journal," he said with a roll of his eyes.

I laughed. "I made it into that journal, thank you very much."

"Did you, now? Well, I need to hear your name then. I'm Charlie, by the way," he said, holding out his hand.

"Vale," I replied, and shook his hand. "It's nice to meet you, Charlie."

"If you're wondering, we have a younger sister named Anne. My parents never once got creative with the names. Guess that's part of Mae's issues."

He made me smile. Much like his sister. "I think Charlie, Mae, and Anne are very respectable names."

He chuckled. "My mother is British. She'd like that comment. She agrees with you."

"Really? I was just thinking you reminded me a bit of Prince Harry."

He cocked an eyebrow. "And here I thought we were going to be friends."

That made me laugh, and laughing felt really good. The tightness in my chest eased, and I took a deep breath.

"Could be worse. You could have said William. At least I'm the rebel son."

I nodded. "A compliment for sure."

He glanced over his shoulder and grinned. "Here comes Mae. She's ready for me to go. I can see it in her eyes."

I turned to see Mae headed our way. "Stop flirting with my potential new friend, Charlie." She paused and looked at me. "Another common, boring name. My parents, gah!"

"He was actually helping me with my empty boxes. They were kind of heavy," I explained.

"Oh, good. He's being helpful. Thank you, now run along. It's time I take Vale here for a good cup of coffee and some of the best ice cream she's ever had."

Charlie shot me a crooked grin. "Have fun, but don't let my

sister teach you too many bad habits. That ice cream will slap the freshman fifteen on you overnight."

"Oh, shut up." She swatted at his arm, then linked her arm through mine. "He's handy to have around, but he can be a pest, too."

I smiled back at him. "Thanks again, Charlie."

He waved. "Anytime, Vale."

Mae snorted. "He likes the brunettes with the blue eyes. It's his thing. And you're petite, and that natural olive complexion is killer. Everything he doesn't have. He's sunk already."

I didn't want him sunk. I wasn't open for anything other than friends. I wouldn't explain that, though. I wasn't ready.

"Are you all unpacked?" I asked her, wanting to change the subject.

"Yup. Now time to introduce you to some people. Who's your roommate? You like her?"

That was a loaded question. "Um, well, her name is Everly and she's very . . . Barbie-ish. . . . She put a pink furry pillow on my bed."

Mae threw her head back and laughed loudly. "Oh, dear lord. They didn't give you a freshman? You got Everly. That's almost cruel. My friend Jasmine, I'll introduce her to you in a bit—she's still unpacking and will meet us later—had Everly last year. That girl is the complete definition of a diva."

CHAPTER FIFTEEN

WALKING INTO THE coffee shop on campus, I expected to see a large crowd of students, which I did. I expected to meet new people, and because Mae was very social I did. But what I didn't expect was the sight of my roommate snuggled up at a table with Slate Allen.

Everly seemed exactly the kind of girl silly enough to waste time with Slate. But still, I just hadn't thought our worlds would be thrown together so soon after arriving on campus. I mean, the place wasn't small.

"Everly with Slate Allen. Not surprised. She had her sights on him last year, but that one is a player. He has a different girl on his arm every day." Mae was talking and I realized I was staring. Just before I tore my gaze off them, Slate's eyes connected with mine and I felt an odd jolt. I quickly turned my attention to the large chalkboard menu hanging over the barista.

What was that jolt? Familiarity?

"Slate is looking at you. I'm telling you, girl, stay away from that one. Nothing but trouble," Mae was whispering. "And now here he comes. Shit."

I tensed, but I wasn't sure why. Slate was a friend this summer when I needed one. He didn't have to keep in touch. It wasn't like he swore he would or anything. I was acting weird about this and I needed to shake it off now.

"Vale." Slate's voice still had a warm drawl. I liked that about him.

Smiling, I turned back to him. "Hey, how've you been?" I said almost a little too cheerily. I wanted to wince.

"Good, and you? Get settled in yet?"

"Oh, you know my roommate, Valerie?" Everly asked as she slid her arms possessively around Slate's.

"It's Vale, and yeah, we're friends," he said, still looking at me. This was becoming even more awkward.

"What can I get you?" the guy behind the counter asked, and I wanted to breathe a sigh of relief.

"Oh, yes," I said, turning to look at him. I hadn't had time to study the menu, so I went with what I knew they'd have. "Whatever you have on bold, please. Large."

"I want a mocha latte with caramel sauce light, large, please," Mae said beside me.

"Six forty-five," the barista said.

I went to get my wallet out of my purse and Mae slapped my hand. "I got this one. You get mine tomorrow."

I started to argue and she rolled her eyes. "Seriously, you got plain old coffee. It was like a dollar. The rest is mine."

"Okay," I relented.

"Let's go somewhere less crowded," Everly said behind me.

"You staying here, Vale?" Slate asked, and the awkward was all over the place.

"Yes, we're meeting some friends," Mae chimed in.

He flashed me a smile. "You make friends fast."

Well, he was supposed to have been my first friend.

"Mae has taken me under her wing," I said honestly.

"Before my brother did. I had to save you," she teased, then turned around and got our drinks.

"I'll see you later, then," Slate said, and Everly stepped between us.

"Bye now," she added.

"Bye," I replied, then Slate turned and followed her out.

"Mother of God, why did you not tell me you knew Slate Allen? Please tell me you've not screwed him."

I almost tripped and jerked my head to look at her. "What? Of course not! He's in my brother's fraternity. We met this summer. Just friends. I'm taken," I added. Because I was.

"Oh," she said, her eyes going wide. "Boyfriend back home? Another college?"

She led me through the crowd, but I didn't see empty tables so I wasn't sure where we were headed.

"Back home," I said without explaining more.

"Those don't always last. You know that, right?" She stopped at a table two other girls were sitting at. "Move over, whores," she said with a playful tone.

"Mae, why were you talking to Slate Allen?" the brunette asked.

"Been there, and stop judging. It's worth it," the blonde said.

"You're a slut, Sam," Mae said, then motioned for me to sit down. "This is my new friend Vale. She's rooming with Everly, God help her, and she's friends with Slate."

"Slate doesn't have female friends," the brunette said, looking at me suspiciously.

"I second that. I've been here as long as Slate has, and he's never had a female friend."

"She's also fucked him," the brunette added.

The blonde who I now knew was Sam rolled her eyes and kicked the other girl. "Shut up."

"So, anyway, these are my friends. Sam and Joy," Mae said, sitting down. "They also have no filter, so I'm sorry for everything that comes out of their mouths."

"Whatever, you don't either," Joy said. "So, tell me, how are you friends with Slate Allen?"

I wasn't sure we were friends, really, but I preferred to use that as an explanation rather than anyone thinking I was one of his many. "He's my brother Knox's frat brother. We met this summer."

"Knox McKinley is your brother?" Sam asked, straightening in her seat.

I was almost afraid to confirm, but I nodded.

"He's gorgeous. I'm angling for an invite to the Kappa Sigma party next weekend just so I can see him. I need to use my new red dress to get his attention."

I was used to girls chasing my brother. This had happened in high school, too.

"Warning, if you try to use or harass Vale over her brother, I will forbid you any contact. No chasing the brothers of friends. Remember my rule."

Sam pouted. "I thought that was just Charlie."

"Nope. Goes for her older brother, too."

Joy chuckled. "Good luck with that."

"I guess I might believe the friends-with-Slate thing now. He wouldn't poach a brother's sister. They're big about that at Kappa Sigma."

Small miracles. I sipped my drink and relaxed a bit. The girls all began talking about their summers and asking me about my life. I left out the fact that Crawford was back home because he was in a coma. I wasn't ready to share that just yet.

CHAPTER SIXTEEN

BECAUSE OF THE blackout drapes that Everly had hanging over the window in our room, I wasn't sure what time it was when I woke up. The room was still pitch black. I reached for my phone. Nine thirty. Wow. I had gotten in bed at ten thirty. I wasn't sure when Everly got in. At least she'd been quiet.

I turned on my flashlight and shined it at the floor so I could find my way to the bathroom. I could get ready before Everly woke up. That way there would be no trying to share the facilities.

"Turn that thing off, Jesus," Everly grumbled.

"Sorry," I apologized, pointing it away from her and toward my baskets by the wall.

"Like, turn it off now," she snapped with loud rustling of the covers.

"I'm just trying to get my things and get to the bathroom," I explained.

"Then fucking hurry!"

I grabbed my basket and turned off the flashlight. I would try to not break an ankle or run into a wall in my attempt to find the correct door. I was afraid of the monster in the bed. She didn't sound like a morning person at all.

I successfully made it into the bathroom and locked myself in before turning on the light. Just in case the light from under the door sent her into a crazed frenzy and she tried to attack. The girl was seriously hard to deal with. I had a pink furry pillow on my bed, for God's sake. What more did she want?

I turned on the shower so the water could heat before I undressed. The steam filled the room and I looked forward to the warm water. The room was chilly. I heard the air conditioner running all night as well as a fan that Everly had plugged in.

Today I was supposed to have lunch with Knox. He'd texted last night. Then I was going to find the library and get the books I needed to start the reading on my course schedule. Mae had mentioned doing something this afternoon. She had to go check in at a restaurant called Polly's where she worked last year as a waitress. They had promised her a job when she returned. She said she'd ask for me. Hopefully I could get a job that easily. My parents expected me to make my own spending money. They'd give me gas money only when I came home. Everything else was on me.

I'd seen two other text message alerts on my phone, but due to having to fight my way in the dark to the bathroom I hadn't read them. I would do that when I was done showering. More than likely it was my mother or one of my brothers checking on me.

I wasn't homesick yet, but I still carried a heaviness in my chest when I thought of home and Crawford. I wanted to call his mom and check on him, but I worried that the reminder that I was here and he wasn't would make her sad. I didn't want to add to what she was already dealing with. I would have my mom get me an update.

After showering, I reluctantly turned off the water and wrapped myself up in my monogrammed towels, one for my hair and one for my body, before reaching for my phone to check my texts.

One was from my mom.

One was from Slate.

I slid my finger over my mom's text first. *Good night, honey. I hope your day was a good one. Love you.*

I sent a quick response about making friends and getting coffee and made sure to tell her I loved her.

Then I slid my finger over the other text. *Good night* was all it said.

I didn't have a response for that. It was morning now. This text came in the middle of the night. I wondered if Everly had even made it back to the room yet when he'd sent it. I didn't have time to think about that. It didn't really matter.

I sat my basket on the closed toilet seat and found my brush. I had a day planned and no thoughts of Slate or dealings with Everly if I was lucky. Neither of them seemed to fit into my life here so far. Everly wasn't the nicest person around. But I typically got along with everyone, so I'd figure it out. Just not right now.

Drying my hair, putting on makeup, and then getting dressed in the dark took all my concentration. By the time I was out the door, Everly had only cursed at me three times. I thought that was pretty good. Considering.

Since I couldn't hang out in my room and read or something until it was time to meet Knox, I headed for the coffee shop to grab some morning caffeine. It wasn't as packed as yesterday, but it was a Sunday so most students were probably still sleeping. Much like Everly.

"You're up early," a male voice said, and I turned to see Charlie standing behind me in line. He had his hands tucked into the front pockets of his jeans and his stance was rather cute.

"It's after ten," I pointed out.

He nodded. "True, but it's Sunday and you should have been living it up last night as your first night on campus. Where's the exhaustion?"

"I guess I missed that memo. I was in bed by ten thirty."

He grinned. "You're a wild one, Vale McKinley."

"That's the rumor," I quipped.

"What can I get you?" the girl behind the counter asked.

I turned back to her and, again, I hadn't had time to study the menu so I went with a regular coffee. At least I was saving money this way.

"She'll also have a shot of caramel in that and a cinnamon muffin with icing. Make that two of each, for here," Charlie said, stepping up beside me and pulling out his wallet. "Breakfast is on me," he added with a wink.

What was it with these siblings? Now I would owe them both a coffee. I wasn't going to complain, though. That muffin sounded delicious.

"Thank you. Next time, I treat," I informed him.

Charlie took the muffins and glanced at me with an amused smirk. "If I ever let a woman buy my coffee, my mother would fly here on her broom and beat me over the head with it."

The image made me laugh. "We won't tell her."

His eyes went wide and he leaned in. "Did you miss the part about the broom? She'll know. She knows everything. I expect to get a call from her later today asking about the beautiful brunette I shared coffee and a muffin with."

I felt my cheeks heat from being referred to as "beautiful." I wasn't good with compliments. Being with the same boy since you were a kid was easy. Comfortable. This was new.

He handed me the two plates with the muffins and he carried

the two coffees as he led me to one of the many empty tables. The one he chose was by a window and the streets were quaint and quiet without all the traffic from yesterday. Oak trees lined the street and flower gardens were everywhere. Even on top of the trash cans.

"I'm going to admit I called my sister last night for details about you. So as much as this seems to be me hitting on you, I'm already aware that you have a guy back home. I won't lie. I was a little bummed, but seeing you here this morning was fate and I think we might just be good friends after all."

That made me relax. I hadn't been sure how to handle things if Charlie asked me out. I didn't want to make it weird between me and Mae. I liked her and I wanted to keep that new friendship.

"I'd like that," I told him, then took a sip of my coffee. I'd forgotten he'd added the caramel, and the creamy taste hit my tongue. I was a fan. "The caramel is great."

He grinned and nodded. "Yep. Only fifty cents more, too. The stuff my sister orders costs almost five bucks."

"Good to know."

"Just wait until you taste that muffin," he added.

I picked up my fork and took a small bite. The warm gooeyness melted on my tongue. "Yum," I said, going for a larger bite.

"The best muffin in town," he assured me.

"I bet this place is packed in the mornings during the week," I said, already sad that I wouldn't have time most days to get either of these things before class. Unless I got up really early. All my morning classes started at eight. I wasn't sure what I was thinking when I did my schedule.

"Line is out the door. I have a hook-up, though. I might share on days when I'm close by."

Smiling at his teasing, I took another bite. Making friends had been easier than I expected. I missed home and I missed Crawford, but I was going to be okay here. When Crawford woke up and was back completely, I'd be able to show him around and we'd experience all this together. He would love these muffins.

"So, tell me about your guy. Is he headed to another college?"

Talking about Crawford was never easy. I had to dance around the actual facts. "He's staying home this year. There are some personal things he's handling. We'll see each other on weekends when I go home, and he'll join me here as soon as he can."

Charlie was listening with his fork paused in midair as if he were waiting on more details. "How long you been dating?"

"Since we were six," I replied, then laughed softly. That answer always got surprised looks.

"Wow, so he's the only guy you've ever dated," he said, as if he couldn't quite believe it.

I nodded. "Yep."

"Jesus, and I thought my three-year relationship in high school was long."

"I definitely have you beat."

He shot me a crooked grin. "You have everyone I've ever met beat."

This was nice. Talking about Crawford and enjoying my coffee. When he came here, people would know him and know our story. It would be an easy adjustment. I looked forward to that day. I just hoped it was soon.

CHAPTER SEVENTEEN

MONDAY CAME AND went in a blur. Making it to each class on time, getting all the first-of-the-semester information, not having time for lunch, then finally crashing in my room with a bag of Cheetos and a Diet Coke around five. Then the studying began.

Tuesday was a replica, but instead of Cheetos it was Goldfish crackers and a bottle of water. I decided to try to be healthier. Which was blown out of the water when Mae brought me a large greasy slice of pepperoni pizza around nine while I was making notes on the evening's reading assignment.

Wednesdays were slower days for me. This morning I had managed to get up early enough to stand in the long line outside the coffee shop. I didn't get a muffin because once I got my coffee, I only had five minutes to get to class. No time to eat. The good news was my afternoon was free, so I'd actually get to eat and catch up on assignments due next week.

Once I was done with all my classes for the day, I headed for the library. Everly wasn't one for studying and she listened to Justin Bieber music loudly and sang off-key whenever she was in the room. I'd pretty much decided the library was going to be my best friend. The only good news was that Everly was out most evenings on dates. I didn't ask if it was Slate, but I'd be lying if I said I wasn't wondering.

I hadn't seen even a glimpse of Slate since the first day in the coffee shop. Nor had he texted again. Which was fine. I didn't think Slate was going to be a good friend anyway. He didn't seem the type. He had an agenda, and friendship wasn't on it.

I went to the fourth floor of the library and found a table in the back behind shelves of books, so it was nice and secluded. No one seemed to venture beyond the second floor for studying, so this seemed like the best idea.

I wasn't sure how much time had passed when I heard giggling, then a deep male whisper . . . then more giggling. I glanced up and looked through the bookshelves in front of me to see the back of a girl pressed up against the other side of the bookshelf.

Slate was the one word I recognized. The girl said his name twice, and then he moaned.

Seriously? Frowning, I tried to block it out and put my focus back on my books.

"That's it," he said with a groan. For the love of God! I glared at the shelves as a few books fell to the ground and he made another pleasure sound. Didn't he have a bedroom at the frat house? I was under the impression that was where this kind of activity took place.

No thank you.

I stood up and took a deep breath before walking around the bookshelves to see exactly what I had imagined. Slate with a girl I didn't know, several books thoughtlessly scattered around them.

Both heads jerked in my direction and I couldn't make eye contact with Slate. I'd now seen enough to know that things would never be the same.

"Um, yes, excuse me, but I'm right over there studying," I said, not looking directly at them. The girl's boobs were exposed and I didn't want to see that, either, so I turned my gaze to my table. "I'm studying and I don't really want to be a voyeur on this whole experience so if you wouldn't mind taking it to, oh, I don't know, your bedroom, the frat house, somewhere that's not a public place . . ." I paused with my cheeks blazing hot. It wasn't like I didn't know what sex was or I hadn't done it with Crawford. It was just that I'd never seen anyone else do it.

"That's what this floor is for. You can move." The girl's voice grated on me.

"I'm pretty sure the school board would agree with me that this is a place for students to study, not screw," I replied, then walked back to my table so I didn't have to continue this conversation with almost-naked people.

"Later," I heard him say. She argued back and then he repeated, "Later."

It sounded like she was having a bit of a fit and I wondered if that was as sexy as the blow job she'd been giving him.

"I said, not right now. Not here." His tone was hard this time.

"You're a jerk," she spat out at him loudly.

"You're the one who begged to come up here and suck my dick," he replied.

A few more books hit the floor, and although the carpet muffled her steps, I could hear her storming off. God, please let him follow her.

The words on the page I was staring at began to blur as I tried to focus, but my heart was pounding nervously. I didn't want him to talk to me now.

"She's right. If you study up here, that won't be the only live sex show you'll see."

Great. He was going to talk.

"This is a library." I stated the obvious but didn't look up.

I heard him laugh, and I suddenly wanted to hurl a book at him myself.

"Yeah, it is. Getting sucked off in the shelves isn't so bad. Kind of hot. Thinking about someone walking up and catching you. Are you a virgin, Vale?"

That got my attention. I lifted my head and stared directly at him. His pants were back up and zipped, which was a relief. "That's not your business."

He shrugged. "The shade of red you were when you saw us makes me think you've not had sex yourself."

I was not going to be made fun of by this man-whore. "I've slept with Crawford."

Slate smirked. "I wasn't talking about sleeping, sweetheart. I was talking about fucking."

Why was hearing him say that word attractive? It wasn't a nice word, but when he said it my heart picked up and butterflies went a little crazy in my stomach. What was wrong with me?

"I need to study," I informed him.

"I texted you. You didn't respond."

Why was he bringing that up? "I was asleep."

"I know. I saw you."

That got my complete attention. "What?"

He closed the distance between us and pulled out the chair across from me. "I came with Everly up to your room. To see you. And you were in bed asleep. You're a cute sleeper."

I hadn't even heard them. I didn't like the idea of them being in the room with me asleep. It was an invasion of privacy. "She shouldn't have let you in the room with me in bed," I snapped, angry at them both.

"I agree. I told her not to do it again."

Again . . . what? "I'm confused."

He leaned back in his chair and crossed his arms over his chest. "Everly is a selfish bitch. So I warned her if she ever let another guy in that room with you sleeping I'd make sure it never happened again."

Oh. I didn't know what to say to that.

"She knows I don't make threats lightly. I rarely make them. But you'll be safe. I promise."

"Why do you care?" I asked before I could stop myself.

He shrugged. "To tell you the truth, I don't know. But I care. That's all that matters."

CHAPTER EIGHTEEN

I'M NOT SURE what happened that day in the library, but something unspoken was said. Things were not the same. Slate started texting me regularly. Not simple *Good night* texts, either. We had actual texting conversations. About classes, Everly's obsessive issues, coffee, the fact I'd had coffee with Charlie again, and even what we were eating.

It was like Slate simply wanted to talk to me. Nothing more. And although it was just texting, we were getting close. Closer than I had ever felt to a guy other than Crawford. Slate was truly becoming my friend.

He invited me to coffee often, met me after classes, and for a week we went to lunch together five times. I liked being around Slate. He made me laugh and he didn't pressure me for anything more than friendship. Unlike Charlie, who had kept dropping hints that he would like to date. I couldn't date. There was Crawford.

Slate took my mind off that pain. When I was with him, things felt better. Happier. Like I might actually find joy again. Deep down, I thought at times about a future without Crawford. Even though it made me feel incredibly guilty, I still thought about it.

For the first time since the accident, I truly had something to feel guilty about. I was living the life we had planned together. I didn't think about Crawford all the time, and my chest wasn't always tight with the pain of loss. Sometimes I would laugh and not realize until later that day that Crawford hadn't crossed my mind. I wasn't proud of it, but I was learning to enjoy life as it was at the moment. Slate was helping me. Mae was too. But Slate was . . . more.

I just wasn't sure what kind of *more* he was. Because although Crawford wasn't with me, my heart was still with him. It had been since I was six. Could that ever truly change?

EVERLY WAS GETTING dressed up for a party at Kappa Sigma that I knew nothing about. It hurt when she told me. The slice came out of nowhere. It wasn't that I was surprised by it. Slate had become my friend. His not inviting me to his fraternity house party made me feel less important to him than he'd become to me. I wasn't expecting an invite as his date or anything . . . but as a friend. At least.

"Knock, knock." Mae stuck her head in the door, glanced around to see the room free of Everly, then smiled at me and came on in.

"She's in the bathroom," I told her before she started talking about her. Mae was not an Everly fan. I didn't know many people who were.

"Who's the hot date tonight?" she whispered, walking over to Everly's bed and picking up the tiny piece of fabric I think was supposed to be her top.

"Not sure. Kappa Sigma party."

Mae turned her gaze to me and frowned. "You're not going?"

It was common knowledge now that I was Slate Allen's only female friend in the history of the world. I shook my head, hoping the hurt wasn't shining in my eyes.

"Jerk," Mae mumbled, then walked over to my closet and began going through my things. I watched her, as she appeared to be on a mission. Until she tossed a pair of black leggings and a strapless silver top that I normally wore under a jacket at me. "Put this on," she said, then started going through my shoes.

"These are leggings," I stated. "I need a longer shirt."

She stood up with a pair of silver strappy heels in her hands and rolled her eyes at me. "No, Rory Gilmore, you do not. Put this on. Get your makeup on and fix that hair. We're going out tonight, too. Screw Kappa Sigma and their dumb parties. Charlie and three of his friends are headed to Linc. We will join them."

"Linc?"

She beamed at me as she got to the door. "It's a college club. Now get ready."

After the door closed behind her, I stared down at the clothing she had picked out for me. There was no reason not to go out tonight. It would keep me from sitting here with my feelings hurt. It didn't take much to talk me into it. I changed clothes, put on some minimal makeup, and used my wand on my hair. Everly still hadn't come out of the bathroom. Luckily my teeth were brushed. It didn't look like I was getting in there.

I checked myself in the full-length mirror Everly had put on the back of the door and almost went back to my closet to change. I didn't typically dress like this. I wasn't completely conservative or anything, but this was tight all over.

The bathroom door *would* have to open just then, and Everly caught me checking myself out.

"Where are you headed?" she asked, sounding surprised.

"Linc," I replied as if I knew exactly what that was.

She raised her eyebrows. "With who?"

"Friends." She was typically nosy.

"Guys?"

"And girls," I added, then picked up my purse and opened the door. "Enjoy the party," I told her. "Say hi to Slate for me." As soon as the words were out of my mouth, I regretted them. I didn't want Slate to think I cared.

I didn't wait for her response. I closed the door behind me and headed for Mae's room, wishing I'd said, "Tell Knox hi for me." That would have made more sense. Not jealous or petty.

I knocked on Mae's door and Sam opened it. "Well, look at you," she said, stepping back. "Looks like Vale has come out to play."

Mae rushed out of the bathroom, then squealed and clapped when she looked at me. "Perfect. We're going to have so much fun."

I hoped she was right. I was in need of fun. I also wanted to forget I'd just told Everly to tell Slate hi for me. So stupid.

My phone dinged in my purse and I pulled it out to see a text from Slate. *Late breakfast tomorrow?* he asked.

I decided I'd ignore that. After a frat party tonight, I figured he'd need a late lunch. Not a late breakfast. Maybe I would, too. I turned my phone to silent and put it back in my purse. Tonight I wasn't going to think about Slate.

"Y'all ready to do this?" Mae asked, fluffing her natural curls.

"Hell yes," Sam replied.

"Then let's go," she said, walking past me to the door and swinging it open.

I had never been to a club. Not one. Ever. I could dance. I liked to dance. But I'd never danced in a club. This was kind of exciting. It was something I thought I'd one day do with Crawford. Again, here I was, moving on and finding a life without him. Every day that passed, the guilt eased and the pain let up. This must be what acceptance felt like. I wasn't sure that was okay.

CHAPTER NINETEEN

THE HOT PINK band on my right wrist told the bartender and anyone else who cared that I was under twenty-one. The black stamp on my right hand told them the same thing. Apparently they were super cautious around here. I guess with college kids they had to be. I didn't mind. It wasn't like I had intended to drink anyway. Although I wasn't sure this stamp was washing off anytime soon.

Charlie and his two friends Drake and Cole met us outside the club. It was obvious that Mae was interested in Drake. He was attractive and tall. He had a bit of a scholarly look about him I wouldn't expect Mae to be drawn to, but she was. Sam latched on to Cole immediately. Which left me with Charlie.

"You look amazing," he said as we weaved through the crowd.

"Thanks. Your sister went through my closet and chose my outfit."

He chuckled. "I'll remember to thank her."

He was flirting. He did that often these days. Which was why going anywhere with him had been getting harder. I wasn't ready to date. Crawford could wake up at any moment, and I wasn't ready to let that go.

"Here's a couple of empty seats," he said, moving me toward

the bar, where there were three empty stools. "You girls can sit while we order drinks."

"Vodka soda," Mae said to Charlie, who wasn't wearing a pink band or a stamp. I had never asked his age, but apparently he was twenty-one.

He rolled his eyes at her. "Try a Coke," he replied.

She glared at him, which only made him laugh.

"Might as well order me a Shirley Temple," she grumbled, then turned her smile toward Drake.

"Don't even think about it," Charlie warned her and Drake. "She's not drinking under my watch."

"Ugh," Mae replied, and crossed her arms over her chest.

Charlie turned to me. "You want a soda?"

"Coke will be fine," I told him.

He then turned and ordered two Cokes and a beer. Guess he wasn't against drinking, just underage drinking. That was respectable and rare.

"You drank your freshman year," Mae shot at him.

He shrugged. "My older brother didn't give it to me, though."

He had a point. But I didn't say so for fear Mae would attack me with the claws she looked ready to attack him with.

The back-and-forth finally stopped and a stool beside me came open, so Charlie sat down. He slid my Coke toward me. "I kind of expected you to be at the Kappa Sigma party tonight. When Mae said you were coming with her I was pleasantly surprised."

I shrugged. "Guess my older brother doesn't want to help me drink or party either."

"I wasn't talking about Knox," Charlie said, leaning into me, his expression serious.

Of course he wasn't. He was talking about Slate. Everyone

talked about Slate and me when we did something together. They couldn't figure us out. Accepting that we were just friends seemed impossible. Maybe after tonight, people would realize it was true. Just friends.

"I'm sure Slate had a date. He wouldn't have wanted to invite me, then feel the need to make sure I was enjoying myself. He'd have his hands full." When I said it like that, it made complete sense and I almost understood his not inviting me. Almost.

Charlie nodded. "So, this guy back home is still a thing then. You're really not seeing Slate."

"Yes, he is still a thing so no, I'm really not seeing Slate. We are friends. Slate doesn't do relationships. I think he's made that obvious."

"You going home to see your guy soon?" Charlie asked. I should have expected that.

I took a sip of my Coke and looked out at the dance floor. I wanted to dance and forget all this. Crawford, Slate, and my silly hurt feelings.

"No, not yet. We are dealing with some things." That was the only excuse I was giving him. It was the only excuse I'd give anyone.

"It happens. Same thing happened to me with the girl I'd dated my senior year. We went different places and lost touch."

That was so not what had happened to me. Not the same thing at all. But then, my story wasn't exactly common.

I took another sip of my Coke and didn't reply.

"If I can't drink, I'm dancing!" Mae announced, grabbing Drake's hand.

I sat my Coke down just as Sam led Cole onto the dance floor.

"You dance?" I asked Charlie.

He grinned. "Hell yeah."

"Great!" I replied, and we made our way onto the crowded dance floor.

This was better. No talking. Just moving to the music. The heartache of my past wasn't being probed. I could forget it all and move.

Charlie didn't touch me too much, but occasionally his hand would land low on my waist and we'd move closer. I always managed to work my way back out of it before it got too comfortable for him. I liked Charlie. He was the kind of guy who could make a girl happy. But for some reason he didn't tempt me. I couldn't imagine a future with him. Nor did I want to.

Mae spun past me, giggling as she pressed closer to Drake. Charlie rolled his eyes and I laughed. They reminded me a lot of me and Knox. I hadn't spent a lot of time with Knox the past two weeks. A lunch here and a coffee there, but that was it. He was a busy guy. Dated a lot more than I realized.

After several songs, Mae went back to the bar for some more soda. I was thirsty, but I was afraid of questions from Charlie I didn't want to answer, so I continued to dance.

"I think you got company," Charlie said in my ear. I stopped dancing to look up at him. He nodded toward the bar and I turned to see Slate leaning there with a bottle of beer in his hand. His gaze was directly on me.

"Why is he here?" I asked, unable to look away from him.

"I think that's obvious," Charlie said, but I wasn't able to look back at him and respond. Slate's focus on me had my stomach doing funny things. There was . . . a thrill. There, I said it. There was a thrill that coursed through me because he was here.

When had my heart stepped aside long enough for this to

happen to me? I couldn't go wanting Slate. That was stupid for any girl. He didn't do relationships.

And neither did I. Because I had a relationship.

"You need to talk to him?" Charlie asked, reminding me he was there. *Crap.* I had forgotten where I was.

"Uh, yeah, looks like it," I finally managed to mutter, then made my way to Slate. Still unable to look away from him.

What was wrong with me? I wasn't this girl.

Or was I? Without Crawford I wasn't sure who I was. Maybe I was exactly this girl. Maybe if I hadn't had Crawford in my life, I would have been this girl. The kind of girl who falls for beautiful playboys who can't promise more than a good time.

CHAPTER TWENTY

I GUESS MAYBE I was that girl.

As I walked toward Slate, I told myself that no, I wasn't that girl. But with each step, part of me wanted to be. Besides, he had to care something for me. He was here, wasn't he? There was a party going on in his frat house and he was here. For me. That wasn't what anyone expected of Slate.

What if he was that guy and didn't know it? What if we had both been lost until now?

"Where's your phone?" were the first words out of his mouth when I was close enough to him.

I hadn't been expecting that question. "Um, my purse," I replied, glancing down to make sure my wristlet was still attached to my wrist.

"Check it."

Check it? My phone? "What?" I asked, still not following this conversation.

He took a sip of his beer, then pointed at my purse with the tip of his bottle. "Check your phone, Vale."

I pulled my phone out anyway and glanced down to see five

missed calls from Slate. "Did you need me?" I asked, looking back up at him.

"I needed you to answer your phone. I get a message from a drunk Everly that you're out at a club and said to tell me hi. Did you think I wouldn't call you after that?"

I didn't think Everly would tell him. I gave a slight shrug. "I didn't think you would. No."

"You're with Charlie again. So you decided you're gonna date?"

I wasn't dating. I was with Charlie and Mae.

"Mae invited me out tonight. Otherwise I'd have been in my room alone all evening. Charlie met us here."

Slate took another drink and studied me a moment. It made me want to fidget. I wasn't sure what he was doing here, but my traitorous heart was hoping.

"Vale," he said slowly with intent in his eyes. "Did you want Everly to tell me you were here?"

Yes. No. Yes. Crap!

I kept my mouth shut. I didn't want to lie, and the truth was impossible to say.

"Why, Vale?" he asked, as if I'd given him an answer.

"Why what?"

He reached over and brushed my cheekbone just under my eye. "I didn't need a verbal answer. Your eyes told me. Now I'm asking you why."

Because I was hurt would not be coming out of my mouth. I had too much pride for that. No matter what girl I ended up being.

Slate grinned and shook his head. "Come on. Tell your friends good-bye and let's go. Just you and me."

The girl I thought I had been would decline and stay here. The girl I was pretty sure had been hiding inside me my entire life nodded.

Mae walked up to us. I turned to her and I guess it was already all over my face. She looked let down but accepting. "Go on. I'll see you tomorrow," she said before I could say anything.

"I'm sorry," I said, because I *was* sorry I was leaving her. I just couldn't tell Slate no. Not when I'd wanted to be with him all night anyway.

"I get it. Go" was her response.

I quickly hugged her and pulled back. "Tell Charlie I said good-bye." I glanced over her shoulder to see him dancing with a new girl. I was glad he wasn't waiting around.

She glanced back at him. "Don't worry about him. That charming nice-boy routine is just that—a routine. He's a player of the worst sort."

I doubted that, but I smiled and turned back to Slate, who sat his beer down then reached for my hand. This was a first. We'd never held hands before. His fingers intertwined with mine, and as innocent as this was, it made my heart flutter and I felt a goofy grin light up my face. I was glad he was focused on the exit and not me. I'd be embarrassed to be caught grinning like a fool.

The night breeze was refreshing after all those people and the smell of alcohol. I inhaled deeply and tried to calm myself. I'd held hands with Crawford all the time. It was something we had done as long as I could remember. But I'd never felt like this when we did. Had I even paid attention to it then?

Slate walked over to the taxi line and held open a door for me. I had been expecting his black Jeep to be parked out here somewhere. "I've had too many to drive."

And once again, Slate Allen didn't add up. He was a frat boy who got blow jobs in libraries, yet when I was around him he was responsible. Another part of him I wondered if only I got to see.

He climbed in after me as I slid over. "Pancake Haven," he told the driver, then looked at me. "We need to talk and I need some food."

"Why did you leave your party?"

He leaned back and stretched out his legs in front of him the best he could. "Because you wanted me to."

That wasn't fair. "I didn't say that."

He chuckled. "No, you didn't. But sometimes, Vale, you don't have to say it for me to get it. You found out about the house party. I hadn't mentioned it to you and you went off to a club where you ignored my text and phone calls. You wanted me to come to you. So I came."

Was he right? Had I done that? I didn't think so.

"Your brother is in my fraternity. I was respecting him. Having his little sister there at a party with drunk guys everywhere would have made him nervous."

"I would have been with you" came out of my mouth before it should have.

"I had a date," he replied.

Oh. Well, that's what I figured anyway. "Where is she now?"

"I left her with a brother."

Now I felt terrible. My ignoring him had messed up his night. Yet he was still with me. Taking me to get pancakes.

"I'm sorry" was all I could say.

"Are you sure?" he asked. He sounded amused.

"Yes."

"Mmmhmmm," he replied with a smirk just as the taxi pulled

in front of Pancake Haven. Slate paid the driver, then leaned over me and opened my door. "I'll follow you out," he told me.

I didn't want to talk anymore. I wanted to go hide in my room for the next four years.

The Pancake Haven smelled of butter, syrup, and fried potatoes. Slate led me to a booth farthest from the door. I didn't make eye contact with him until the waitress walked up and asked us what we wanted to drink. I went with coffee, since I figured I wouldn't sleep much tonight anyway.

"I don't date, Vale. I hook up. It's the way I do things," he said as the waitress walked off.

I nodded. I had nothing to say to that.

"You and me . . . we click. I enjoy being around you. I like you. I liked you this summer in the hospital. But you're a dating kind of girl. All you've ever known is a relationship. I can't do that."

"Why?" I asked before I could stop myself.

He sighed and leaned back in the booth. "Because it's not me. I like freedom."

He was honest and I had no right to judge. "Okay."

He cocked an eyebrow. "Okay, that's all you're going to say?"

I shrugged. "What else is there to say?"

He ran his thumb along his jawline as he studied me. "I still want to see you."

"We're friends. We can stay friends. Just because I think I may eventually be ready to date doesn't mean I can't be your friend, too." Where had that come from? Seriously, had I just said I was going to date? What was wrong with me?

A frown line appeared between his brows. "Date?"

I was as surprised as he was. But I continued blabbering words I didn't know I felt, yet they flew out of my mouth just the same.

"Yes. I think . . . I think it is time for me to date. I don't know when Crawford will wake up. He wouldn't want me to live frozen. I don't plan on getting serious with anyone, but I think I need to date. He's all I've ever known."

"So who are you going to date? Charlie?"

I shrugged. I doubted after I left him tonight that I'd be dating him. All I had thought about was wanting Slate earlier. But that had been cleared up when he made sure I understood he wasn't dating.

"I don't know," I replied as the waitress set our coffee down in front of us.

"Have you decided on what you want to eat?" she asked.

"No, give us some more time, please"—he paused and checked her name tag—"Mary," he added.

She smiled and blushed. I didn't blame her. "Okay," she said, her voice going a little high-pitched.

"You've only ever been with Crawford. You have to be careful who you go out with. Guys can't be trusted." He sounded so earnest and sincere. Like he was telling me something vitally important, and I needed to get it.

"I'm not putting an ad in the paper or anything," I replied, slightly annoyed.

"This is serious. Trust me on this. If you're going to date, then at least let me clear him first."

I wish I could have laughed at that. But the fact that he had just sounded like one of my older brothers stung so badly, I wasn't sure I could take a deep breath. The first guy other than Crawford who I'd developed feelings for saw me as a sister. Until tonight and this moment, I hadn't been able to admit I had feelings for Slate.

I hadn't been ready for all this to hit me at once. I needed to leave. I slipped my clutch back on my wrist.

"I, uh, get it. I have four older brothers. I don't need a fifth. But I'd like to go home. You stay and eat. I'll . . . uh, catch up with you later."

I barely looked at him while speaking, then slipped out of the booth and hurried to the exit. I needed an escape. There was no taxi line out here, so I just started walking. When I got far enough away I would call Mae. Or Google a taxi number. Something. I just wasn't staying here.

CHAPTER TWENTY-ONE

"VALE!" I WAS expecting that. My dramatic exit was simply because I needed to get away from him before I burst into tears. But I knew he'd come running after me. I had just hoped I'd get farther before he could pay and chase me.

I stopped walking because he would catch me anyway. Staring ahead at the dark road leading toward campus, I took several calming breaths and tried to tell myself I hadn't just acted like an idiot.

"What the hell?" he said as he slowed from his run to stop beside me.

The hell was I liked him. A lot. I wasn't used to this. That was what the hell was.

"I was worried about you. Did I miss something or does my concern give you reason to run down the fucking interstate in the dark?" He threw his arm out toward the road I was headed on. Oops. Guess I hadn't been going toward campus.

"I don't need another brother," I blurted out.

"You mentioned that. But I'm not trying to be a brother. Not even close."

That made my chest ease a little. Not enough.

"I'm capable of choosing the right guys to date," I added.

He looked skeptical. "This is your first time. I just . . . I just want you safe."

"Why, Slate? Why do you care? Why did you bring me coffees, and text me, and come around? Why did you make me like you? *Why*? What was your purpose? To prove you could and then let me down?" I really hadn't meant to say all that, but it gushed out anyway.

He stared at me like I was speaking another language. Did he really not see that he'd done just that? It all started with that damn coffee in the hospital.

"You needed coffee and you were alone. I wanted to do something to help."

That was all he was going to say to all I'd just thrown at him?

"Well, you helped," I said bitterly. *Maybe too much.* I started walking again. This conversation was pointless.

"Where are you going?" he asked.

"To my room," I replied.

"We're about ten miles from the dorm."

Well, crap.

"I'll get us a taxi," he told me, and instead of walking into the dark all alone I stopped and turned back around.

"Fine."

"Vale," he said with a sigh. "Don't do this."

"Do what?" *Be honest? Was he against honesty?*

"You know what. I like us. We work. I just can't be more than what we are."

"What are we, Slate?"

"Friends. Really damn good friends."

Fine. That was what we were. I could live with it. This was a part of the dating years I never experienced. Wanting a guy who didn't return the feelings.

"Okay. Then, friend, can you get me back to my room? I really want a shower and my bed."

He pulled out his phone and made a call. When he was finished, he nodded back to Pancake Haven. "We need to go wait there. That's the pickup."

I started walking back feeling silly and hurt all at once.

"This isn't going to change us, is it?" he asked, walking too close. He smelled good.

"No," I said, wondering if that was true.

"You're important to me, Vale. I didn't plan on that, but you are."

"Okay," and I wanted to say, *You, too*, but I didn't.

The taxi came fast, so no more awkward conversation about things staying the same. I got out my phone and sent Mae a text along with Charlie. Then I checked my e-mails and Instagram to keep busy. Luckily Slate didn't try to talk.

When the taxi finally pulled up to my dorm, I slipped my phone into my purse and forced a smile before looking up at Slate. "Thanks for the ride. See you around." That was the best I could do.

The best he could do was let me go. And he did.

WHEN I CRAWLED into bed about an hour later, I picked up the photo of me and Crawford by my bed. "I miss you," I whispered. Then I opened the drawer on my bedside table and slipped it inside. Tonight I would cry. For Crawford and all we lost. And for finding someone else who I could have loved, but who would never give me the chance.

It is a weird thing to mourn a relationship that never was. I didn't know this could happen, but it was real, and it was painful. When I woke up it would all be fresh. A new day. A time to find myself and learn to be happy. Life had dealt me some difficult cards, but I was going to find my own path now.

I didn't need a guy to complete me. I never did. I just never had the opportunity to find that out. Until now.

CHAPTER TWENTY-TWO

OVER THE NEXT week Slate texted a simple *Hey, what you doing?*

I had waited hours to reply. Finally I texted, *Studying.*

And that had been it. No more small talk or attempting to keep things as they were. They had actually never been much. He had made sure to not let me get too close.

Focusing on my classes and finding a job had become my way to get through the week without thinking about him. Too much. The job search wasn't so difficult. Mae had hooked me up easily enough and tonight I started my first shift. They were throwing me to the weekend crowd on my first night, but Mae would be training me so I wasn't too nervous.

The uniform for Polly's was black shorts that I wished were a few inches longer and a tight blue T-shirt that said POLLY'S BAR AND GRILL on the front. I had asked for a looser shirt, but Mae had explained that Polly herself wanted the shirts tight. It kept the male customers happy. There were televisions all around the place playing different sports and there was beer. I didn't see why we had to dress a certain way to make men happy. They had beer, burgers, and sports. What more did they need?

Mae told me not to complain—the outfit helped with the tips. I was thankful that I had a job and I was getting to work with my friend.

The night started off easy enough. I followed Mae around and watched her work. The computer system for putting in the orders was the only thing that made me nervous. I took mental notes each time she used it, hoping I would get it right when I was doing this by myself. I wanted to start writing these notes down, but that didn't seem like a good idea. Especially when Mae didn't even write drink orders on paper. She just remembered them.

Seven tables and two hours into the night I was relaxing a bit when Mae turned to me and smiled. "There's a table for you to take on your own. It'll be good practice."

I wasn't ready for a table alone and I started to tell her that when my eyes met Charlie's and I understood. She was letting me practice on her brother and his friends.

"Oh. Okay. I think I can handle them."

Mae smiled, nodded in their direction, and walked into the kitchen. I pulled out the little notepad that she had given me, which I had never seen her use. I wasn't ready to memorize orders. I had to remember how to work that computer first.

Charlie saw me headed his way and his smile eased my nerves even more. I recognized Drake and Cole. They had another guy with them I didn't know. His hat was turned around backward and his attention was on the football game.

"Hello," I said, smiling. "Can I get y'all some drinks?"

Charlie leaned back, still grinning from ear to ear. "I'm a fan of the outfit."

I rolled my eyes. "I'm not."

"Mae been teaching you the ropes?"

I nodded. "Yep. Y'all are my first table without her, so if I mess stuff up, forgive me."

"We're a good group to train with. Unless you get Cole the wrong beer—then he'll be nasty," Drake chimed in.

"Don't listen to him. I'll forgive any mistake," Cole replied.

"You ran off last weekend. Left Charlie here all high and dry," Drake decided to add.

I glanced back at Charlie. I was sorry I'd left. He hadn't deserved me running off with Slate like that. "I know. I was rude. I shouldn't have left."

Cole chuckled. "Sounds like someone found out the hard way just how Slate plays."

"Shut up," Charlie snapped at him.

"What can I get y'all to drink?" I asked, now wanting to change the subject.

They each ordered a beer except Charlie, who ordered a Coke. I wrote it down and headed back to the computer to put it in. I couldn't fix the beer—the bartender had to do that. But I'd need to handle the Coke after I had it in the system.

"You good?" Mae asked, coming up beside me.

"Yeah," I assured her.

"They'll be a good table for you to practice with. I'm here if you need me."

"Thank you," I replied. I was more than thankful for Mae in my life.

She nodded, then headed back into the kitchen.

They ordered appetizers next, then burgers. It was all pretty easy and my confidence was building. I enjoyed this. Getting a job wasn't just a necessity, but it was going to help fill my free time. I didn't need to be thinking about Crawford or Slate.

Maybe fate has a funny way of handling things, or maybe it just likes a good laugh. Heck, I was beginning to wonder if it just hated me in general. Somewhere in my life I'd made an enemy of fate.

I was about to give Charlie his Coke when I saw Slate sit down a few tables away. He was with a girl. I stood there staring at them. I needed to look away and accept that this was going to happen a lot. The ache it caused me was ridiculous. I hated that.

Before he could turn his head and see me gawking at him, I jerked my gaze away and swore to myself I'd not look at him again. Focusing on my table was all I intended to do.

"Here you go," I said, trying to sound happy.

They barely tore their eyes off the television to mumble their thank-yous.

"Y'all need anything else?" I asked, hoping they would say yes so I would have something to do.

"Yeah, bring me that brownie with ice cream," Charlie said. Then the table echoed their wanting one, too. So, four brownie delights. I didn't write that down. First thing all night I hadn't written down.

When I got to the computer, Mae met me there. "Ignore his ass," she said in a disgusted-sounding whisper.

I shrugged. "Not worried about that."

She smirked. "Yeah, right."

Okay, so she knew me better than I realized.

"He was a bad idea," I told her. "And I'm done with bad choices."

"He was a bad choice that most girls make at this school. You figured that out before the others do. Like the one he's with tonight—she'll be crying tomorrow night when he's off with another one. It's how Slate Allen does things. A girl goes out with him and she has to know it's just for sex."

I was glad I hadn't slept with him. I didn't want to be that girl the next day. Being the girl I was now was hard enough. If I wasn't jealous of the girl he was with tonight, I would feel sorry for her.

"I need to put in four brownie delights," I said to change the subject.

Mae nodded. "Okay. Just ignore him," she added before walking off and leaving me to the computer.

Once I had the desserts ordered, I decided to go back into the kitchen and wait for them. But not before I glanced over just once . . .

Only to catch Slate watching me.

CHAPTER TWENTY-THREE

THE ONE THING I could be proud of tonight was that I didn't stand there and stare back at him. I quickly turned away and went into the kitchen like I had intended. He was on a date. He needed to be staring at his date.

The desserts were ready a little too quickly, but I couldn't hide in the kitchen forever. I placed them all on a tray and headed back into the dining room. Charlie saw me coming and I focused on him. From the look on Charlie's face, I was pretty sure he'd seen Slate, too.

He probably thought I was one of Slate's many after last weekend. I didn't want that, but leaving with him had been my mistake. Something about spending time with a guy in a hospital made you trust him more than you should.

"These look good," I said as I began placing the brownies in front of them.

"They're fucking fantastic. Want a bite?" Cole asked.

"I better not. You enjoy that."

I could feel my back was rigid, and I hated that Slate just being here was making me react this way.

"You okay?" Charlie whispered when I placed his brownie in front of him.

I forced a smile and nodded. "Yep. Can I get y'all anything else?"

"Milk," Drake said. "I should have ordered a glass of milk before. Sorry."

"Drink your beer," Charlie told him, sounding irritated.

"No, I agree milk would be good with this. I'll get it. Anyone else?" I needed something to focus on.

"Well, if you're getting him one, I want one, too," said the new guy I didn't know.

Charlie grunted as if he was put out with them both.

"I'll be right back," I assured them, and hurried into the kitchen. I felt like I'd scored a victory by not glancing toward Slate.

I went to the large commercial fridge and got out the open gallon of milk to pour into two glass mugs from the freezer.

"He left," Mae said, startling me. I missed the mug, spilling some of the milk over my right hand, then finished filling them. I didn't want to respond to that.

"Left a twenty on the table to cover their drinks, then left," she added.

I picked up the mugs and turned to look at her. "Guess they didn't like the menu." Then I headed out the kitchen door. I had to look this time. Even though I knew he was gone, I had to reassure myself. It was weakness, but I glanced. And Mae was right. He was gone.

THE REST OF the night Mae didn't bring up the Slate thing. She got the hint I wanted to ignore it, and being a good friend, she played along. I worked behind her after my only table for the night left. The rest of the night went fast. On the way back to the dorm, we stunk up Mae's car with the scent of fried food. I couldn't wait to get a shower.

"You did good tonight," Mae told me as we got out of the car.

I took a deep breath of air, hoping to cleanse the greasy smell from my nostrils. "Thanks. It wasn't so bad."

Mae nodded in agreement. "It's good money and we get to work together."

"We just stink of food when the night is over," I added, and she laughed.

"True. Soon you'll get over it, though, and it won't be as bad."

I doubted that. I started to say so, when I noticed a figure standing by the door and paused. It was late, and I didn't trust what looked from here like a man standing outside a girls' dorm late at night.

"What?" Mae asked when I didn't move forward.

I started to point out what I saw when he moved, and I could easily make out Slate's face in the moonlight. Why was he here?

"Nothing," I told her. "I thought I forgot my phone in your car, but it's in my purse."

"Oh," she replied, not sounding very convinced. Slate moved around to stand even farther back in the shadows before we got to the door, and I barely cut my eyes his way before following Mae inside.

I'd like to say I was going to go right up to bed. Slate was probably here for some other girl. But after him ignoring me for a week, coming to the place I worked on a date, and now this, I was ready to tell him exactly what I thought of him. Especially since guys like Charlie thought I was one of his many castoffs.

As Mae headed to the elevator, I turned toward the steps. Once I knew she was out of sight I headed back outside.

Slate was there waiting.

"Why are you here? Was tonight not enough? There are three other women's dorms on this campus. Can't you go screw someone in one of those? Do you have to keep showing up where I am and flaunting your dates in front of me? Does that give you pleasure?"

"Fuck," he muttered, and then his hands cupped my face and his mouth was over mine.

This I had not expected.

But my body didn't seem to have a hard time keeping up. My hands slid up his arms and held on while my mouth opened to his, and he took that invitation to deepen things.

My heart pounded in my chest as my knees went weak. I didn't know knees could actually go weak from a kiss. But mine were. And I couldn't get enough. His lips were soft and warm, moving over mine as if I were an instrument and he knew exactly how to play me.

I'm not sure how long I let this go on before reality sank in and I realized I was kissing Slate. I'd never kissed anyone other than Crawford. And when I did, I picked a guy who had just been kissing some other girl he'd taken on a date. That was the cold water I needed to wake me up.

Jerking back, I covered my mouth and took several deep breaths. I was in shock at me and at him. This didn't make any sense. I knew better than this.

Neither of us said anything. We just stood there staring at each other. What could we say? Had he been here for me? No. He'd been on a date. And he had just kissed me. What kind of guy did that? Slate Freaking Allen. That was who.

"I can't believe you did that," I snapped at him, dropping my hand from my mouth and stepping back.

"Why?"

Was he kidding? Why? God, did this guy have no morals at all?

"Oh I don't know, Slate! Maybe because you are on a date! Waiting on some other girl!" I yelled, pointing back at the entrance to the dorm.

"No, Vale, I'm not. I was here waiting on you."

Oh.

I stood there thinking about that a moment before responding. Did I want him to wait on me? No. I didn't want my name attached to his as one of his many one-nighters. It may already be, but I didn't need to make it worse.

"Why?" I asked.

"I don't know. I just needed to see you. Talk to you."

"You were on a date tonight," I pointed out.

He shrugged. "That doesn't mean I don't miss you."

Well, it meant he was confusing me. Completely.

"Slate, what is this? Why are you doing this? You want to be friends, then you just ignore me. Now you show up here missing me. I didn't go anywhere. You chose to stay away from me."

He sighed and ran his hand through his hair. "I know."

This conversation was frustrating. I had worked all night and I wanted a shower and my bed. I started to go back inside.

"Vale, don't. Please." His voice was what got me, more so than his words.

I stopped, and with hesitation looked back at him.

"I don't know what . . . how . . . you're different. I want to see you, every day. But I can't do a relationship. That's not me."

It was me. But it was me with Crawford. Not me with someone else. I wasn't ready for a relationship with someone other than Crawford yet. How could I demand something I wasn't prepared to do? Crawford would eventually wake up. I wasn't giving up hope of that. Then what?

"I can't do one, either," I said simply.

"I understand that."

Where did that leave us? Was I just supposed to accept him dating a different girl every night and still do things like date him and kiss him? Could I even do that?

"Can we date? Just not exclusive? See each other more?" He paused, then a small smile touched his lips. "And I want to touch you. I fucking dream about touching you."

My heart slammed so hard against my chest I lost my breath for a moment. He wanted to touch me and the images suddenly running through my head were taking over. I wanted that, too. So I decided right then that yes, I could do that. It was all I could promise too. Asking for more was unfair when there was Crawford. Each day he didn't wake up made it seem more real that he may never wake up. The longer he stayed in the coma, the worse the outcome. But I wasn't ready to say that he never would. I wasn't letting him go. Even if I realized now that things with us hadn't been perfect. I had done so much to make him happy. I had changed me. I wanted to be me again. There was a chance he may not want that when he woke up. But I knew now I had to stop letting him make all the decisions.

"Yes," I replied. I didn't think about the repercussions or how I'd feel when I saw him with other girls. At that moment I just thought about how it felt to be with Slate and that my sadness seemed to dissipate when he was around.

He closed the distance I'd put between us, then placed his hands on my waist to pull me closer to him. Before I could even take a deep breath to calm my racing heart, his mouth was back on mine and I was holding on to his biceps again for fear my knees would give out on me.

This was enough. It was all either of us could promise the other right now. Or ever. That made my heart twist and I couldn't think about why. Facing my feelings for Slate meant accepting things were changing for me. If Crawford woke up, I would go back to him. That was what I did know.

CHAPTER TWENTY-FOUR

BREAKFAST? WAS THE text that woke me up the next morning. It was Saturday and after ten, so it was time for me to crawl out of bed anyway.

I'd replied *Yes*. And then got up and quickly dressed. In the dark. Like always.

Slate met me outside my dorm with a cup of coffee twenty minutes later. After last night I wasn't sure what to expect next, but this had not been it. His slightly-too-long dark hair was tucked behind his ears, and he wore a tight gray T-shirt with the Kappa Sigma crest on the front. The jeans he was wearing weren't bad either. He definitely turned heads when he wore them.

"Morning," he said with a sleepy smile. It was well after ten now, but it was still too early for him.

"Good morning and thank you," I replied, taking the coffee.

"Sleep good?"

I nodded and took a sip. I had actually slept really well. I wasn't sure if it was exhaustion or my decision to date Slate.

"You good with going in to Nashville and getting something to eat?"

The only other good breakfast place around here was the

one where I had run out on him, and I didn't want to remember that.

"Sure," I replied.

"I need to go see my uncle, too. He's back in the hospital. The chemo has been hard on him. Want to ride with me? Maybe stop by and see your folks?"

That I hadn't planned on. Going back home and facing Crawford and my memories. I missed my parents and seeing them would be nice. Slate needed to see his uncle, and he obviously didn't want to go alone.

"Okay," I said before I could talk myself out of it.

"I'd like you to meet Uncle D. I told him about you this summer and he's curious."

"You told him about me?" I asked, surprised.

"Hell yeah, you were the most interesting thing happening up at the hospital."

I had told Crawford about him, too. While I talked to him at night. I decided not to bring that up with Slate. We walked out to his Jeep and he opened the door for me. Again. Something Crawford had always done. Something I didn't expect from Slate.

"Thank you," I said, feeling almost ashamed that I was so surprised by this.

He smirked as if he knew what I had been thinking, then went around to his door and climbed in. His Jeep smelled of him. His cologne. I liked it in here.

When he pulled out onto the road, I glanced over at him and decided I didn't really know much about him at all. He knew much more about me. But then, he'd asked. He'd tried to find out. I'd done nothing like that.

"Have you always lived with your uncle?" I asked.

"Since I was six. My dad ran off on my mom shortly after I was born. Never knew the man. And my mom died from a bad case of pneumonia when I was six. She didn't have medical insurance and one day she just didn't wake up. Her older brother was her only living relative and he came to pick me up."

While he was telling me, my chest grew tight and began to ache. "How long were you alone with her before someone came to check on you?" I asked through the lump forming in my throat.

"When she didn't wake up for a whole day I called 911. She'd taught me if I thought something was wrong and she couldn't help me to call 911. I often wonder if I'd called sooner if they could have saved her. But I was just a kid. Uncle D helped me work through that guilt."

All I had known was security. It's all I'd ever seen. In my life and in Crawford's. Now Slate was watching the man who had raised him slowly die and it seemed so unfair. He'd suffered enough.

After the accident I had been so focused on Crawford that I never considered how easy our lives had been until that moment. To me, nothing could have been as terrible. Yet it could have. Things could always be worse.

"You were smart to call 911. I don't know if I'd have thought to do that at six," I admitted.

He shrugged. "You would have. I think kids think things through and make smart decisions before adults do. Oftentimes adults panic and react poorly."

There was so much I didn't know about Slate, but the more I heard, the more I respected him. Sure, he liked to sleep around and he was aware that his good looks could get him his way, but his life hadn't been an easy one.

"So you began working on a farm when you moved in with your uncle?"

He nodded, then grinned like it was a fond memory. "Yeah. Uncle D doesn't believe in feeling sorry for yourself. He had me out learning to feed the chickens and getting their eggs the day after my mother's funeral. I hadn't even started my new school yet or unpacked in my new room. I worked two full hours on his farm before I got to go inside and get ready for school. It was hard work, but I think it was what got me through those first few months. Losing my mom, moving five hours away from the only life I knew, a new home, a man I hardly knew being all I had—it was a lot for a six-year-old to adjust to. The work on the farm helped me. I didn't sit and think about it too much."

When I was six, I was playing with dolls and begging to go to the park. The ice cream truck would come down our street playing its music loudly and I would meet Crawford outside to go get an ice pop. It had been a storybook life where nothing bad ever touched us.

"He sounds like a good man," I said simply.

Slate chuckled. "Yeah, he is. He also uses foul language and says whatever he's thinking. His temper is terrible, but he never hurts anyone. Just yells and fusses a lot."

I looked forward to meeting him. Seeing another part of Slate's life. The more I knew, the more I realized just how special he really was. That was probably dangerous talk and I didn't need to think of Slate as special. But I did . . . because he was.

CHAPTER TWENTY-FIVE

WALKING BACK INTO the hospital where I'd spent most of my summer was more difficult than I imagined. The things I'd been able to put out of my mind while I was at Bington were resurfacing. Like the night we'd come here after the wreck, and being told Crawford was in a coma. Not memories I liked to think about.

I wanted to see Crawford while I was here. Even if it wasn't a scheduled time Juliet was prepared for. I was past letting her make all the decisions.

Every other nurse we passed waved, winked, and called out a hello to Slate as we passed. I was trying not to count them, but it was hard when it never seemed to end.

"Wipe that judgmental expression off your face. I didn't fuck all of them," he said a little too loudly as we stepped onto the elevator.

"I don't have that expression on my face," I argued, and he just laughed and shook his head.

I probably was making a face.

"Now you're frowning," he added, still grinning.

I glanced up at him. "Why are you watching my face?"

"Because it's cute."

Oh.

The elevator door opened and my thoughts went to meeting his uncle. This was important. I already respected this man. No matter how many times he cursed while we were in there.

"Uncle D was a big man once. The cancer has slowly beaten his body down. But when I was a kid, he was like the Incredible Hulk to me. He could do anything. It's hard to see him so frail now."

Slate was preparing me, or maybe he was preparing himself. The little boy in him needed reminding that the big man he knew wasn't there anymore. The lump threatened in my throat again and I mentally scolded myself. I couldn't get emotional. He needed me to be strong.

"Here we are," he said, knocking on the door once before turning the knob and going inside.

"It's about motherfucking time you got your sorry ass down here to see me. Hell, boy, I could be dead in a week." A deep voice—not one I imagined from a frail man—filled the room.

"Stop your bitching. I'm here, ain't I? And I brought something nice to look at."

I stepped around Slate to see a man you could tell once had a big build, but his body was thin and pale now. The sickness had taken so much of him. His pale blue eyes met mine and he began to smile.

"Well, Jesus, Mary, and the cradle, it's a woman that ain't half-dressed and hanging on your arm like a common prostitute."

"Uncle D, this is my friend Vale McKinley. I told you about her this summer. Her boyfriend is the one in a coma. Vale, this is my uncle D."

He continued to study me. "How's that boyfriend of yours? Opened his eyes yet?"

I shook my head. "No, sir. He hasn't."

He frowned. "Well, he better fucking hurry that shit up before you get hitched to someone else. Pretty girls like you don't stay single long."

"Have you eaten today?" Slate interrupted him.

His uncle shot him a disgusted look. "I ain't saying nothing I shouldn't. Stop trying to change the subject. And no, I ain't eatin' that shit they bring me. Pure ol' horse dung would taste better."

He turned his weak gaze back to me. "Now, you don't go getting any ideas about this one." He raised his gnarled hand and pointed at Slate. "He ain't for the likes of you. He can't stay with just one. Not in him. Sure as he realized he had a face that made women's panties fall off, he started using it. Shame, it is. A good girl like you would be the thing to give him the life he always liked to pretend he had."

"You gotta eat something," Slate said. "What do you want? I'll go get it."

This time I had to cover my mouth from the giggle that bubbled up when Uncle D rolled his eyes before looking back at Slate. "Boy, if'n I want something to eat, I'll tell you. Now stop being so goddamn rude and let me talk to this girl. She needs some wisdom from an old geezer like me who has seen it all."

Slate sighed and walked over to the sofa under the window and waved his hand for me to have a seat. "Might as well get comfortable. I don't think he's close to easing up."

I went over and sat down beside Slate. His uncle was entertaining, and I liked the way he and Slate bantered with each other.

"Now, tell me about school and how you're both doin'. It's important to get the schoolin' or you'll end up like me, working on a farm your whole life."

Slate leaned back and crossed his arms over his chest. "I'll let you go first," he told me.

"It's harder than I was prepared for, but I've been spending a lot of time in the library." My cheeks heated at the mention of the library, and I hoped he didn't notice. Thinking about Slate and the girl in the stacks wasn't the mental image I needed at the moment. "It's helped get my mind off everything else, though."

Uncle D turned his gaze to Slate. "And you, boy? You still fucking in the library or you studying, too?"

A laugh burst out of me and Slate just shook his head. "You're not even gonna give me a break with company here, are you?"

Uncle D raised what would have been his eyebrows if he hadn't lost all the hair on his head and face to the chemo. "You thinking she don't know? Hell, she's heard it all about you, I'd wager. It's a miracle she's seen in public with you."

"We're friends," Slate informed him.

Uncle D made a huffing noise and waved Slate's comment away. "Ain't nothing about that girl meant for friendship. You see her and you want her. She's just too good and clean for ya. Or that's what you think. But hear me now, 'cause I know what I'm talking about. That girl wouldn't be here with you visiting your sick dying uncle if she didn't care about you. So you get that shit out of your head and be smart. Be fucking smart for once. Don't let the thrill of a skirt and easy sex mess this up for you. The best sex ain't easy. You just don't know it yet."

If my face could get any warmer, I would be surprised. I knew I was blood-red. The heat radiating off my cheeks was enough to warm the room.

"Okay, that's enough," Slate said. "Let me get you something to eat. I think we've had enough wisdom for the day."

But his uncle D wasn't finished. He looked at me. "He's been a whore. I'll be the first to tell you. But that ain't affected his heart any. That boy's got the biggest one I've ever seen. When he loves, he loves big. He doesn't let you down and he stands by you no matter what. I know it because he loves me. Don't let his past mistakes and possibly his future mistakes let you miss out on being loved by a heart that damn big."

CHAPTER TWENTY-SIX

THE AWKWARDNESS FROM Uncle D's advice had eventually faded when he began talking about the hot nurse that hadn't been in today and how he'd eat peanut butter and crackers if she'd feed him.

I enjoyed being around Slate's uncle. He was right: Uncle D had no filter and said whatever he was thinking. Every time I remembered he was sick and dying, my heart ached. I didn't like to think of him being gone. The love and respect in Slate's face when he looked at his uncle was obvious. It also made complete sense as to how Slate had turned out the way he had.

Next we headed for Crawford's room. I wasn't sure what made me more nervous—having Slate with me or Juliet's reaction to the sight of me.

"Why don't you go on in alone? I'll get a Coke and wait out here." I could argue with him that no, he should come, too, but I didn't. Because the idea of him coming with me was part of what was making me nervous. It wasn't like Crawford would see us together and know something. It just . . . it was cheating. At least, that's what it felt like.

"Okay," I agreed. He squeezed my hand.

"Go see him. Talk to him. I'll be waiting."

That. That right there was what made Slate special. It was hard to pretend he wasn't special when he did things like that. What guy was so understanding in a situation like this? I hadn't known one.

I knocked on the door lightly before slowly opening the door and stepping inside. Juliet was, of course, sitting by Crawford's side and a book lay open in her lap. Her eyes locked with mine and her eyebrows rose in surprise.

"Vale, I didn't know you were home," she said, studying me.

"I'm just here today. I wanted to come see him. I should have called. But it was a last-minute decision."

She seemed to be okay with that. Thank goodness. "I'm sure he'll be happy to hear your voice. Knox was here a few days ago and read to him. I think he had more brain activity. He needs voices other than mine."

I walked over to the side of his bed. "He looks good," I said, not really meaning it. He was thin. Nothing like the muscular athlete he had been. It was hard to see him like this. I wanted him to open his eyes and look at me.

"Yes, he does look better these days. I think he's getting ready to wake up soon." The hope in her voice was clear. I hoped the same thing, but saying it was difficult.

She stood up. "I'll let you talk to him. I need to go get something to eat anyway. Take your time."

This was different. Very unlike her, but then, I wasn't camping out in the waiting room anymore. I nodded.

When the door closed behind her, I looked back down at Crawford. So many memories. Where once I had thought it was all good things, I knew now that there were memories that weren't so good. Like the way I had changed for him. Without meaning to. That would never be the same. When he woke up, I wasn't doing that again. I loved him. He was a part of every memory I had of growing up. But I had to be me. And he had to love me for me.

"College is a lot like we imagined. I've made friends. You'd like them. You'd like everything about Bington. It was a good choice. I'm glad you picked it. Even if I hadn't been on board at first."

He lay there sleeping. So I talked more. "I miss you, but I'm finding a way to move on. To live. Life without you seemed impossible at first. I wasn't willing to even try. But I knew you'd want me to. So I am."

I looked around the room that had become a part of his life. His existence. "You'll wake up soon. Things will be different. For both of us. I'm worried about that. Even a little scared. I'm not the same girl I was on graduation night. And I know you won't be the same, either. This isn't exactly what I imagined when we talked about growing up."

Again, nothing. Just the silence. I stood there and watched him breathe until his mother returned with a bottle of water in her hands. Saying good-bye was easier than I thought it would be. My life was truly changing.

ONCE WE WERE back in the Jeep, Slate didn't ask me questions about Crawford. Nor did he mention anything his uncle had said. I had actually expected him to do both, but he acted as if there was nothing to talk about. So I went along with it. He was quiet, and I could tell seeing his uncle so sick was hard on him. Leaving him had seemed to be the most difficult.

My parents were expecting us, and so was the rest of the family, apparently, because all their cars were parked out front when we pulled up. I had given my mom a call after breakfast to let her know we were visiting Slate's uncle and Crawford, then stopping by to see them. She insisted we eat dinner with them.

Slate had seemed on board with the idea. The only one missing was Knox, who was back at Bington. He worked Saturday nights at a local radio station. I also didn't let him know I was going anywhere with Slate. I had seen and heard enough already. I didn't need his warnings.

"So it seems that the rest of the family will be joining us for dinner," I said, feeling like this was a bit unfair. Slate hadn't agreed to the whole family thing. "My brothers and I are close. They aren't used to me being gone all the time. Jonah you won't see tonight because he's a Marine and on active duty. But the others are all here."

Slate nodded and smiled, but the smile wasn't as genuine as it had been before we visited his uncle. It had been hard on him. Again, I wanted to hug him and tell him it would be all right. But the truth was, it wouldn't be, and we both knew it. His uncle D's time was limited.

"It's okay. I like the McKinley family members I've met so far. I'm sure everyone else is just as cool."

They were. I loved my family, and after spending the day with Slate and his uncle I realized I was incredibly lucky to have the large family I had. No sickness had touched us. No death. Crawford had been the biggest tragedy we faced. And I still believed he would open his eyes one day.

"Okay. Well, the food will be good. More than likely one of my favorites. You can expect red velvet cake for dessert."

"Momma's baby has come home for a visit," he teased.

I nodded. Because he was right. "Yep."

I opened the door and waved him inside. "Here we are."

The house wasn't huge. It was big enough for us, though. The foyer had a coat rack that currently held two rain jackets, an umbrella, Mom's purse, and her reusable shopping bags. The stairs were right around the corner leading up to the four bedrooms. One for my parents, one for me, one that Knox and Jonah had shared, and one that Dylan and Michea had shared. They all still remained the way they had been left when the others had moved out. Except there was a baby bed in Dylan and Michea's old room. The girls had outgrown the baby bed, but it was waiting on the next grandchild.

Voices from the kitchen and living room were so loud they hadn't even realized we were here. This was typical of my family. Everyone was always trying to out-talk the others.

"VALE!!" Maddy was the first to see us. She screamed my name and ran at me with her arms up in the air.

I bent down to catch her just as my mother, father, Malyn, and Catherine all came out of the kitchen. Michea and his fiancée, Hazel, came from the living room with Dylan.

"I didn't even hear y'all come in," Momma said, wiping her hands on her pink polka-dot apron that the girls had painted for her last Mother's Day.

"I expect not with all the talking that was going on. Everyone, this is Slate Allen. He is a friend of mine and one of Knox's frat brothers," I said. Then I turned back to Slate. "You've met Dylan and the girls. This is Catherine, Dylan's wife and the girls' mother." I then went on to make the rest of the introductions.

Dad shook his hand, as did Michea. When I was finished, Maddy decided to remind us that she'd seen him kiss a nurse. He was never going to live that down with the girls. Dylan had quickly hushed her up, and I smiled over at Slate. He needed to be careful where he kissed people.

The table was already set and I was sure Mom had put Catherine and the boys to work as soon as they got here. We had a long, wide farm table that my dad had made just after he and Mom got married. We filled it up now, and over the years he'd had to make two benches for either side to fit everyone.

Right down the middle was where the food was placed and we passed it all around to fix our plates. I scooted in to sit beside Maddy and let Slate take the end seat. "How's your uncle?" my mother asked as soon as plates were filled and everyone was comfortable.

"He's tough," Slate said, "but he's not getting better."

Mom looked at him in a way only a concerned mother could. "Well, we are here if you ever need us to take him something. Meals, or just to check on him. Don't hesitate to call. I was thinking of sending Dylan up there with a plate tomorrow. We always have so many leftovers."

"I'm sure he'd like that. He hates the hospital food. His appetite isn't much these days."

Mom nodded, and I was willing to bet that Uncle D got a hot meal from her every day from now on. She, however, never mentioned Crawford or asked about my visit with him. I figured Slate's being here had her keeping quiet about that.

"I was hoping Knox could make it home tonight. He didn't have time to stop by the other day and it's not easy with y'all both being gone," Momma said, looking down at her food.

"Yeah, me and Michea aren't enough to keep her happy. If Michea and Hazel would hurry up and get hitched and shoot out some kids, then she'd have something else to worry over. The girls are getting too big now, and she needs a baby to tend to." Dylan was teasing, but there was truth to his words.

"Leave your momma alone. She's doing just fine. We're all glad Vale is off at school and living her life again. Ain't no one wishing she hadn't gone," Dad piped up before soaking his corn bread in turnip greens and taking a bite.

"How are classes?" Catherine asked me, changing the subject before the boys could keep on.

"Good. Harder than I was prepared for, but I'm managing."

"So how is Knox adjusting to the frat house life?" Michea directed his question to Slate.

The rest of the dinner went just as smoothly. Slate laughed at stories my brothers told about my childhood, and although some were very embarrassing, it was making Slate laugh so I let it go.

WHEN WE LEFT, both my parents told Slate to come back anytime. That he didn't need me to get a good meal. For that, I hugged my parents. Simply because they had no idea what they had offered him. Something he'd never really had. A big family.

CHAPTER TWENTY-SEVEN

EVERLY WAS NOT happy. It wasn't a guessing game as to why she was angry, either. I was a good roommate. I overlooked the pitch-black windows when the sunshine should be lighting the room so I could see to get dressed, and the fact I had no space in the bathroom for my things, and the way she left her shoes and clothing draped all over the place—even my bed at times. Heck, I even accepted the furry pink pillow and ridiculous paintings she hung around the room.

So she had no reason to be mad at me. But she was. And it was all because of Slate. He had begun picking me up in the morning and walking me to my first class. I didn't think much about it, other than it was really nice and saved me from going without coffee, because he always brought me some. However, the rest of the dorm was buzzing about it, because Slate Allen didn't do this.

But he was doing it with me.

Telling people we were just friends didn't seem right, either, because we were dating now. Not exclusively, but we were dating. I tried not to think about the exclusive thing too much. I didn't want to know who else he was seeing. For now, he seemed to be seeing only me.

WHEN I CAME out of the bathroom the next Friday morning, Everly stood at the door with her hand on it like she wasn't going to let me leave the room. She was normally in bed at this time yelling at me to be quiet.

"Why you? What, do you have a magic vagina or something? Do you give world-class blow jobs? I mean, what is the deal here? I am a hundred times more attractive than you. I am fuck-worthy. *Look at me!*" She waved her hand down her body as if I should be taken in by the sight. "So why is he seeing you over and over again? Slate Allen doesn't do that. He is a one-time fuck. Everyone knows that."

I knew the guy of whom we spoke was waiting on me downstairs. He had just sent me a text.

"Move, Everly. I have a class to get to."

Her face grew bright red and she slapped the door. *"Answer me, damn it!"*

I'd seen her pitch fits before, but this one was on its way to being her worst yet. "Possibly because I don't act like this."

She looked confused. "Like what?"

"A psycho bitch. Now move."

"Did you just call me a *bitch*?" she roared loudly. I was beginning to wonder who all could hear this and if a crowd had gathered outside our room to listen.

"Don't forget the *psycho*. That's really important."

Her eyes flashed pure hate, and I wondered if I had gone too far. I had never in my life been in a fight and I didn't want to have my first one now.

"You'll regret that. I always get what I want. *Always.*"

That was a threat that didn't even make sense. What did she want? Slate? She was in for disappointment.

"Noted. Can I leave now?"

She rolled her eyes and stepped away from the door.

When I opened it, three of the girls down our hall were standing there with big eyes, listening. I had figured as much. This would be all over campus by lunchtime. I'd have to tell Slate about it. As silly as it was.

Slate held out my coffee as I climbed into his Jeep. "You're late."

I was typically very punctual. "Everly" was my explanation before I took my first drink of coffee.

"Getting ready in the dark again," he said, already knowing my normal Everly woes.

"Nope. I have that mastered. Today she got up to threaten me about you. She's not happy about this," I said, pointing at the two of us. "You aren't supposed to see a girl more than once."

Slate chuckled. "Yeah, she's a bit wack. That's why it took me a year to even give in to her constant flirting and just get it over with."

"Very romantic," I drawled.

He shrugged. "That's me. Mr. Romance."

I smirked and sipped more coffee. I wasn't rested enough for this class and I had a full day, then work tonight. I would finally be working without Mae, and I was nervous but looking forward to the tips.

"You working tonight?" he asked, and I nodded.

I almost expected him to ask what time I got off, but he didn't. He stayed quiet and we drank our coffee in silence. When he drove up to the building that was my stop, he leaned toward me. "Come here."

I met him halfway and he kissed me. The kind I'd come to expect every morning. The kind that made it hard to walk to class with his taste on my tongue and his scent still surrounding me. This was my favorite part of the morning.

"I'll see you later," he whispered against my lips as the kiss ended.

All I could do was nod. My breathing was still a little erratic. The best way to snap out of this was to think about how kissing Crawford had never made me feel this way. It was what I had finally come to acknowledge while walking to my morning classes. It sobered me and reminded me that my life was changing. I was happy again. Without Crawford.

I hadn't thought that was possible. To enjoy life without him. But I had my memories. Our childhood was a good one and those memories would always be there. Sometimes life throws changes our way that make us stronger and show us we don't always know what is best.

Sitting down in class, I got my laptop out of my book bag so I could get settled before the professor arrived. I had a routine. Set up my laptop, sign on to the Internet, and get my coffee in the right spot.

"She isn't the only one. He's taking Babs to the Kappa Sigma party tonight. All she's talked about all week is Slate Allen asking her out. I think they're just friends. Maybe she's a lesbian."

The whisper had been a mock one. The girl wanted to act as if she didn't want me to overhear her, but the pitch in her voice said she definitely wanted my attention. If that was meant to hurt me or upset me, she had succeeded. Not because Slate was doing anything wrong—he had made it clear that this wasn't exclusive. Simply because for me he was it. I couldn't kiss him and then go date someone else. I didn't want to. But he did. That hurt.

This was something Crawford never would have done. I'd asked for this. I'd accepted it. But I wasn't sure I could actually do it.

CHAPTER TWENTY-EIGHT

WHEN SLATE TEXTED me about meeting him for lunch, I gave him the excuse that I had a study group I needed to be at. He didn't argue and I didn't say any more. I even stayed at the library until the very last minute before changing and heading to work in case he came by the dorm to see me. I wasn't prepared to see him. Not with knowing he had a date tonight but kissed me this morning.

He'd have sex tonight. That was what he did. I knew this, yet I would kiss him every morning and in the afternoon when I saw him again. But how many of those times had he left me and gone to screw someone else? He hadn't tried to do anything but kiss me. He had a reputation for wild, hot sex, but he never touched more than my hand when he held it, my face when he kissed me, and sometimes my waist.

Maybe he wasn't sexually attracted to me. That had to be it. I thought he liked kissing me, but I was beginning to see that maybe it had been to make me feel better. Maybe the kissing didn't affect him like it did me. He wasn't overcome with lust and the need to do anything more. Tonight he would, though. He'd take her to his room and screw her. She'd tell everyone and I'd be his lesbian friend.

Fantastic.

My phone buzzed and I glanced down to see a text from him asking me where I was. I thought about ignoring him but decided against it. I told him I was headed to work.

He didn't say any more. Good. I didn't want to keep responding to him. It wasn't easy. I wanted to throw my phone every time I saw his name. And I shouldn't even be mad at him. It wasn't his fault. Just because I wanted more and he didn't. At least he'd been honest about it.

Luckily, my first night on the floor alone was so hectic I didn't have time to think about frat parties or Slate Allen. I was too busy remembering drink orders and how customers wanted their burgers cooked.

Pocketing three hundred dollars and forty-five cents in tips after tipping the bartender and busboys was nice. I hadn't expected tips like that, and although Mae had warned me that Friday nights were better than the other nights of the week, I still liked the money. I needed to work every Friday night.

That wasn't the only unexpected thing that happened that night. Only the first.

When I stepped out the back door to go to my car, Slate was waiting on me. He was leaning up against the front of my car with his arms crossed over his chest and a serious expression on his face. He was supposed to be at his frat party. With his date.

I stopped and stared at him a moment. I wasn't sure I wanted this confrontation. He would only be here if he knew that I knew about his date. What, had he already screwed her and left her? Was he that shallow? Thought he could just come running to me afterward?

"Why are you here?" My words were angry. I couldn't pretend otherwise.

"Because I wanted to see you."

I shook my head and walked around him to my car door. "You saw me. Now go back to the girl good enough to fuck and leave me be." *Ouch* . . . that was not what I meant to say. The words were just flying out of my mouth without thought or hesitation.

"What is that supposed to mean?" he asked, and that only made me angrier.

I jerked open my car door with way more force than was necessary and glared at him. "It means that I've changed my mind. I can't do this." I paused, then finished. "Whatever this is. I am not that girl. I will never be that girl."

My next course of action was to get in my car and drive off. Unfortunately, Slate was faster than me and he was behind me with his hands on my arms, stopping me before I could move.

"You can't do what, Vale? Say it! What is it you can't do?"

He wanted to hear it. *Fine.* I shook him off me and spun around. "I can't be the girl you keep around because you don't want her sexually while you go screw everyone else. I can't let you kiss me and then go sleep with some girl that turns you on. I don't do it for you. I'm not enough. FINE! I quit. I have more pride than this. I—"

Then his mouth was on mine and no more words were coming out. I put both hands on his chest to push him away, but he grabbed my wrists and held me there while he kissed me like I was his last breath. Like he couldn't get close enough to me. And it only took a few seconds of this intensity to melt into him and run my hands up his chest and into his hair.

Slate's hands slid to my waist, then they moved lower, covering my bottom and jerking me flush up against him. The hard thickness that he pressed into my stomach was something I knew. I recognized it, and it told me one thing was certain: I did turn Slate on.

I rubbed up against him, wanting to feel it. Feel him. The groan that came from his chest sent shivers through me, and I held on to his hair and tried to get even closer.

His right hand slid down my thigh, then jerked it up by the knee until I was open to him. Until his hardness was pressing where I needed it most. I cried out against his lips and moved my hips so that the friction from the contact gave the pleasure my body was aching for.

"Fuck," Slate muttered against my lips as he broke the kiss and began pressing a trail down my neck and toward my chest. My breaths were short and gasping with each inch he drew closer to my breasts. I wanted this. I wanted it with Slate. I didn't care anymore about who he'd been with before. I just wanted him.

"Vale," he whispered as he lifted his head to look up at me. I couldn't speak so I just met his gaze. "Get in my car."

I nodded, but my legs weren't sure they could work. Slate picked me up and walked back to the dark area of the parking lot to his Jeep. Stopping at the passenger door, he dropped me back to my feet and pressed me up against the cool metal. "Let's get something straight. I've wanted to fuck you since the moment I laid eyes on you. The fact I didn't was out of respect, not lack of desire. You're different."

Oh.

Then his mouth was back on mine and his hand was at my shorts, unbuttoning them with smooth efficiency. We were in a parking lot at my place of work, and when my shorts began to slide down my legs, I waited until they hit the ground and stepped out of them. Slate fell to his haunches and picked them up, then ran his hand up my bare leg until he reached the top.

I held my breath as he leaned in and kissed the pink satin of my panties. That was something I'd never done with Crawford. We had just had sex a couple of times. Like everything else with Slate, this was different. It was life-changing.

CHAPTER TWENTY-NINE

SLATE MOVED ME against him as he opened the door behind me and then backed me up before picking me up and setting me in the seat. He slipped my panties down and tossed them onto the backseat, then placed a hand on each of my knees and slid them open. Exposing me to him. Something else I'd never done.

"I gotta taste you," he said with a hoarse whisper, before lowering to his knees and sinking his head between my legs. The first swipe of his tongue had me crying out his name and grabbing his head. That was unlike anything I'd ever had. I wanted more.

The more he kissed me there and ran his tongue in places that ached for him most, the more desperate I grew. His name was the one thing I managed to cry out as my body sped tighter and higher toward release. I was willing to accept anything if I could feel like this.

Just as I thought I was going to scream and pull out all Slate's hair, my world exploded and the release shot through me. I was left trembling as he kissed up my stomach, then pulled me into his arms. "You enjoyed that." His voice sounded pleased and I gave a weak laugh.

"Yes." I stated the obvious.

"I did, too. And for now I'm going to let that be enough."

Wait. What?

"Don't be mad. I like you all soft and relaxed in my arms. I'm taking it slow with you, Vale. You are different. I don't want to treat you like the others. I can't. My feelings . . . I just . . . I can't."

Could this be enough? Being with him like this and knowing he was with other girls, too? The idea of him touching someone else like he'd just done to me was breathtakingly painful. I wouldn't be able to handle it.

"I can't, either," I said, pulling away from him. "That was amazing . . . but I can't be with you this way and know I'm one of many."

Slate sighed and took my face in his hands. I liked it when he did that. It was like he was claiming me. Telling me he cherished me. Wanted me. "You are the only one. I haven't been with anyone in two weeks. The more I'm with you, the more I want to be with you. Just you. I can't even stand being near other girls because they aren't you."

I wanted to believe that. It was beautiful. But it was a lie.

"I know about your date tonight."

He nodded. "Yeah. I figured. But did you know I canceled it this morning after I kissed you and dropped you off? I didn't want it. I just wanted you."

Oh.

He pressed a kiss to the tip of my nose. "It's just you, Vale. For the first time in my life I'm not looking. I found what was missing."

My heart squeezed and I felt tears sting my eyes. I didn't want to cry, so I buried my head in his shoulder and inhaled. I felt safe. But more than that I was happy. Complete. And he wasn't Crawford.

"Are you crying?" he asked, his voice sounding amused.

I shook my head, thankful no tears had fallen, and then looked up at him. "No."

He smiled down at me. "You're so fucking gorgeous it's distracting. Getting past all that and finding out you're beautiful inside. That there's this world you see through your eyes that I want to see. And I get to when I'm with you."

"Thank you," I said, emotion clogging my throat again.

"For the epic pleasure, or for being completely infatuated with you?" He was teasing me again.

"Both," I whispered, feeling my cheeks heat up from his blunt descriptive words.

"In case you were wondering, you taste as good as you look," he added, slipping a hand under my shirt, then down to cup my still-bare bottom.

Giggling, I buried my face in his neck again.

"God, you're cute, too. I'm completely sunk."

I was glad he was sunk. I didn't want him going anywhere.

GOING TO SLEEP that night was hard. The smile on my face as I stared at the ceiling thinking about all he'd said and our good-night kiss felt right. Even with Everly coming in at two in the morning stumbling drunk and cursing at me, even though she thought I was sleeping. I hid my smile from her.

I wanted to tell Mae, but I hadn't wanted to wake her up. She was already figuring out my feelings for Slate. That I wanted more than the friendship that I had claimed. Admitting this to her was going to be fun and make it seem real. I felt as if I were in a dream at times. Especially now with Slate.

CHAPTER THIRTY

SLATE WAS AT one of my tables watching football the next night when Knox walked in and went straight to him. I hurried and got the drink order out to the new table I had, then went directly to them. I hadn't talked to Knox about things with me and Slate in a week. But with Slate missing the party last night to be with me and then sitting at one of my tables while I worked, it was obvious that things were different. We were a couple.

Slate was listening as Knox talked. The serious expression on my brother's face made me get a little panicked. He didn't need to step into my business. I knew what he thought of Slate. And I knew how wrong he was.

"Why are you here, Knox?" I asked, not even trying to hide my irritation.

"Talking to Slate is all" was his easy response. He was full of crap.

"Yeah, right. You planning on eating or you about done?" I asked him.

He held up a hand. "Calm down, sis. I'm just chatting with him."

I hated it when he talked to me like I was a child. "And I'm asking why?"

He leaned back in his seat. "Because rumor has it y'all are in a relationship and I've never seen Slate in a relationship. It's all you've ever known. I don't want you hurt."

I started to open my mouth when Slate beat me to it. "I'd never hurt her. I couldn't. She means too much to me."

Just like when he kissed me and when he said the sweet things to me last night, my knees felt weak and my heart did a pitter-patter thing.

Knox turned his attention to Slate. "Is that so?"

"Swear it," Slate said with no question in his tone.

Knox looked back at me. "You want this? With him?" I knew what he was saying. He was asking me about Crawford. My entire life I'd been with Crawford. It was what my family expected. How did I explain this to him?

"Yes. People change. Life changes."

Knox stared at me as he turned over my words. I knew he understood what I was telling him. Finally he nodded. "Fine. If this is what you want."

"It is."

"Then bring me twelve hot wings with a Coke."

That was it. We were done. And he was staying to eat with Slate. Letting out a relieved sigh, I nodded and turned to get his order in and check on my other tables.

That was a confrontation I had dreaded, and I was glad it was over. I didn't want to have to defend this thing with Slate to anyone. Especially my family.

A couple of the other waitresses noticed Slate not leaving my section and asked me about him. Some knew him and others wanted to. Mae kept looking at me knowingly as we passed and I knew I had to tell her. She was my friend.

When Knox parked himself beside Slate for the evening, Mae finally came over to me and put her hands on her hips and raised both her red eyebrows. "Well?"

"We're dating. Exclusively," I told her, not needing more than the "well" to know what she was talking about.

Her eyes went wide and she glanced back at him. "Slate Allen is exclusive? For real?"

"Yep."

"Holy shit," she muttered. "I thought maybe you were going to sleep with him tonight or something stupid like that."

"We decided on the exclusive thing last night. It's . . . we're different."

She let out a bark of laughter. "You're telling me. Slate Allen doesn't date exclusively. Y'all are definitely different."

I nodded, unable not to grin.

"So that's why Knox is here. I was worried we were going to have a fight over your virtue or something."

"Just doing the annoying big-brother thing."

"Charlie is going to be so bummed."

I hadn't talked to Charlie in a week. He knew I was interested in Slate. It had been hard to hide. We had actually discussed it when we had met up for lunch two weeks ago.

"Uh-oh. You got trouble," Mae whispered, staring back at Slate's table. I turned to see Everly and one of her friends sliding in beside Knox and Slate.

Slate's eyes lifted and met mine immediately. I knew he hadn't encouraged this, but I hoped he'd handle it. I saw him talking to Everly sternly while looking at me.

She leaned into him and put her hands on his chest and Slate was up and out of his seat fast. He said something about her being desperate and walked off, leaving my brother there with the two girls. Knox was grinning.

I remained where I was until Slate got to me. He wrapped an arm around my waist and tugged me to him before kissing me thoroughly right there for the entire place to see.

"I'll be outside in my Jeep waiting until you get off," he whispered, then pressed money into my hands before walking away.

I could feel the daggers that Everly was aiming at me, but I didn't care. I was smiling like a fool and watching his swagger as he exited the place.

"Oh my God," Mae said as she came up beside me. "Sam will never believe this."

I didn't really want to think about Sam or anyone else Slate had slept with in the past. Instead I wanted to think about what he'd just done. It wouldn't be the first time he would have to do that. He was Slate Allen, and women expected him to be open. I hadn't really thought about how that would work until I saw it in action.

When I turned around, Knox's gaze met mine and he gave me a slow grin, then a small salute. It wasn't his complete acceptance, but he was saying he would be okay with it. I didn't need his approval, but it did make things easier.

Everly was now flirting with Knox and trying to act as if Slate pushing her away and walking off on her hadn't happened. Although I was pretty sure the whole place had seen it. She was really going to hate me now. I might need to start sleeping with one eye open. Or at least wait until she came in drunk and passed out. Which was almost every night. It was amazing the girl was passing her classes.

"Let me finish up that table," Mae said. "I don't want to have to hit a bitch for you while we're on the clock. And if you go over there, she's gonna say something stupid and I'm gonna have to kick her skinny Barbie ass."

I agreed. It was best I didn't speak to Everly.

CHAPTER THIRTY-ONE

THE GOOD NEWS is Everly didn't come back to the dorm that night. I finally stopped looking for her somewhere between one and two when I dozed off. The next morning when I saw her bed empty, I opened the drapes and let the sunshine in. Strange how you miss something like sunshine in your room in the mornings. It takes not having it at all to realize you love it.

It was Sunday and I didn't have work tonight. So, Slate was picking me up to go on a hike through Mossy Ridge Trail and take a picnic lunch. I liked the idea of getting away from Bington and being alone with Slate. I also loved hiking. It had been something I did with Crawford. I wanted this memory with Slate, too.

I was ready to start building those memories with Slate. Just as I was ready to move on from the ones I had with Crawford. Each day that passed and he didn't wake up was one more step away from what once was.

Slate met me downstairs with a bag of muffins and coffee. I had ordered the lunch from a deli in town that we would stop and pick up on our way.

"Good morning," he said, leaning in to kiss me.

"Morning," I said against his lips.

"Did the wicked witch give you any trouble last night?" he asked when we pulled apart.

"Didn't come back. I got lucky."

He nodded. "If she gives you any trouble, let me know. I'll handle it."

Smiling, I took my coffee from him. "Are you going to beat her up for me? It's frowned upon for boys to hit girls, you know."

"I'm aware of that rule, but I have ways to make sure she doesn't mess with you."

I didn't ask what, because I wasn't sure I wanted to know.

"That's very double-O-seven of you," I teased, and opened the bag to get out a banana nut muffin.

"I try," he added, and held out his hand for his chocolate-chip muffin.

"We need to stop by the deli on Sixth Street. The one with the pink flamingo outside. I ordered our lunch from there. They even pack it up in a basket."

He laughed. "We'll look like serious hikers with our picnic basket."

I shrugged. I wasn't concerned with looking serious. "It'll be good and the other hikers will be jealous."

"And that's definitely all that matters," he agreed.

"Yep."

After we finished eating and picked up our lunch, we had about a twenty-minute drive to the place we were hiking. I liked driving through Nashville. I had grown up right outside the city, and going into town had always been a big deal. The little kid in me came out every time I drove through.

"Uncle D called this morning. They're sending him back home. He said Jeffery, his neighbor and good friend, was planning on checking in on him and Wilma, Jeffery's wife, said she'd keep him fed. Still worried about him going home like this, but Jeffery and Wilma are good people. I'm going to give them a call this evening. Check on things."

Being away from his uncle while he was sick like this was hard on him. I could see it in his eyes—the concern and the worry. I wished there was something I could do, but I was at a loss.

"Maybe we could drive up next weekend? I could ask off work and we could go to Huntsville for the whole weekend. You could make sure he has everything he needs."

Slate stopped at a red light, then looked over at me. "You'd do that?"

"Of course," I quickly replied.

He smiled at me then and leaned over to give me a quick kiss. "Thank you, Vale. That means a lot."

"You're welcome."

We drove in silence the next few miles, then pulled into the parking lot by the path that was marked for hikers. "The whole loop is only about five miles. It's a rough path, though. Might want to unpack that really cute basket and put it in my backpack instead. It'll be easier for us to carry."

"I think that's a good idea," I agreed, and moved our lunch.

"You've got good hiking boots," he noted as he looked down at my feet.

"My family is big into hiking" was the only reason I gave him. I didn't want to explain that this was something I once did with Crawford. I wanted today to be about us.

"Uncle D and I hiked a good bit, too. Especially when I was younger."

"Did you hike this trail with him?" I asked as he slipped his backpack on.

"Yep. About ten times probably."

That was good to know. At least he knew where we were going.

"Let's do this," I said as he locked up his Jeep and slipped the keys into the side pocket of his bag.

There was only one other car parked out here, so we weren't going to be passing many people along the way. I was happy about that.

We talked about past hikes and told funny stories, and stopped to see different spots of pure, natural beauty. Once Slate stopped to pull me against him and kiss me, saying he just couldn't look at me any longer and not at least get a taste. When he did things like that, it made me feel silly and giddy inside.

By the time we had worked up an appetite, we were at a landing with a few scattered tables and a beautiful view of a stream with fish swimming between the rocks.

"This is our spot," he said, putting the backpack on a table.

"I'm starving," I admitted, and began unpacking the chicken salad sandwiches, fruit, potato chips, and brownies. I was glad I'd ordered several sandwiches because I could eat two at this point, and I was sure Slate could eat that or more.

"How many of these do I get?" he asked, reaching for a sandwich.

"I'm taking two. So the other three are yours."

He leaned over the table and kissed me one more time before we sat down to eat.

CHAPTER THIRTY-TWO

THE DAY WAS perfect. The more time I spent with Slate, the more I admired about him. The love he had for his uncle was obvious, even though his life there hadn't been easy. He'd been taught hard work. Something I really hadn't experienced in my life. Neither had Crawford.

We were almost to the curve that I knew was going to lead back to the parking lot when Slate's hand slipped around my upper arm. Stopping, I looked at him, confused.

"You hear that?" he whispered.

I went very still and listened, but I didn't hear anything. So I shook my head.

He tugged me closer to his chest, then bent his head down close to my ear. "Listen. You sure?"

I was beginning to get a little nervous. I knew there were bears out here and I didn't want to meet one up close and personal. But as hard as I listened, I didn't hear anything other than the water from the stream and a few birds.

"I don't hear anything unusual," I finally said as quietly as I could.

He nodded. "Good. Me, either." Then he settled his hands onto my hips and pulled me tightly to him before covering my mouth with his.

The smile that tugged at my lips was reciprocated by his own smile. He'd tricked me, but I liked this kind of trick. Kissing Slate was something I thought about often. Today it had crossed my mind at least every thirty seconds. He had the kind of mouth that made you think about kissing.

When he pulled back, his heated gaze was locked on mine. "You trust me?"

I did. Completely. So I nodded.

Then he reached for the hem of my shirt and pulled it up and over my head, leaving me standing there in my sports bra. "I want to see all of you."

The way his voice went all deep and thick when he said it made it impossible for me to think that getting naked in a public place was a bad idea. Again, I followed his lead. Because I wanted it, too.

I slipped the sports bra off and tossed it to the leaves at our feet. I couldn't meet his gaze again, though. I felt my chest flush as my hands went to my leggings. He didn't let me get that far, though, before his hands were cradling my face and he was kissing me again.

I leaned into him and my breasts brushed his chest, causing me to shiver from the contact. The only thing that could have been better was if he was also shirtless. I reached for his shirt, and grabbing handfuls, I began to pull it up until he stepped back just enough to let me take it completely off him.

This time, when I pressed against him the warmth of his skin sent delicious tingles through me. His groan of pleasure made me try to get even closer. This was so much more than I had ever imagined. Being with Slate was exhilarating. It felt right. Like nothing else could ever be this perfect.

His hands went to my pants and began tugging them slowly down my hips, until we had to break the kiss for me to slip off my boots, let the leggings fall to my ankles, and step out of them. I was only in my panties now, and Slate stood back. His nostrils flared as he took me in.

"You're too good for me. I've known it since the moment I laid eyes on you. Too perfect, too beautiful, too untouchable."

No. I wasn't. I wasn't perfect at all. I reached a hand out and began to unsnap his hiking shorts. "I disagree," I said simply.

His hand covered mine and he said my name in a sigh. "If you do that, I'll want more. It's taking all my self-control not to grab you and press you against that tree and lose my fucking mind just from being inside you."

The way he said it wasn't pretty, but they were real words. Descriptive words—and I wanted it. My body was pulsing for it. "Please," I said without any fear. Because I didn't fear Slate. I trusted him.

"Vale," he whispered in a choked voice. I continued with his shorts until they were at his feet. Then I began tugging my panties down as I watched him. I was being brave. I was being more wanton than I'd ever been in my life. Even with Crawford I'd never been this brave. When we'd had sex, it had been shy and almost awkward at times.

I was naked outside with a man and I wanted it. This was different.

He finished undressing himself, then paused. He reached for his shorts and pulled out a condom from his wallet. I didn't question that. This was Slate Allen. And I was thankful he was pre-pared. Protection had been the last thing on my mind, but know-ing he was trying to keep me safe meant something.

He scooped up his discarded shirt, and then picked me up as he began kissing me again, walking us back to a picnic table. When he set me down on my feet, he placed his shirt on the table, then put his hands on my hips and lifted me onto the shirt. "I imagined this. A million fucking times. Each time, you were some-where special. Not on a picnic table in the woods."

His words made me smile. I couldn't think of anywhere more perfect. I leaned forward and pressed a kiss to his lips. "This is ex-actly what I imagined," I teased, making him chuckle.

"God, I want you." His voice was harsh as he pulled me tightly against him, pressing my breasts flush against his chest. My thighs opened, and I could feel his erection pressing exactly where I needed it to be. "Please," I begged, lifting my hips.

He slipped inside me then, and I knew my world would never be the same. I grabbed his arms and threw my head back as he filled me over and over again. The sweet friction and heat from his body made me crazy for more.

"Fuck," he groaned as I rocked my hips hard against him, need-ing it all. That was the only invitation he needed to make his thrusts deeper, with more power. Exactly what I needed. I told him so and he said my name in a hoarse whisper.

I lifted my legs to press my knees against his hip bones and he slid even farther inside me, making us both cry out.

"Fucking heaven," he said, grabbing my hips and getting rougher with me as his eyes dilated to the point that the green was gone. He looked like a man lost to his own pleasure, and that sent me over the edge. I fell back on my hands and lifted my hips as I screamed his name, and I'm pretty sure God was mentioned too as my body was racked with wave after wave of euphoria.

Slate's roar of release was the sexiest thing I'd ever heard. His fingers bit into my skin and I hoped they left marks. To remind me how beautiful this was.

When my breathing finally slowed, I was being gathered into his arms as he slowly pulled out of me. I wrapped my arms around his back, and we stayed like that for several seconds. I couldn't imagine anything ruining this moment. It was even better than I'd expected.

"I'm in love with you." Slate's words should have shocked me. But they didn't. Not after that. I had felt it. This was the change in my life I never saw coming. It was the gift I didn't know I wanted. My path had just turned into something different. And I was happy.

If only this moment could last forever.

But eventually, like with all good dreams . . . you have to wake up.

PART TWO

I wake to sleep, and take my waking slow.
I feel my fate in what I cannot fear.

—Theodore Roethke, "The Waking"

CHAPTER THIRTY-THREE

VALE

IT WAS BLURRY. What was blurry I don't know, but I had a hard time focusing. There were noises around me I didn't understand and I felt strapped down. Opening my mouth, I tried to say something, when I heard a voice shout loud enough to leave a ringing in my ears.

"She's awake!"

Who's awake? I wondered. Then, in my vision, I saw someone I knew. A face that gave me reassurance. My mother.

"Vale? Sweetheart?" Her voice was becoming clear and she was talking softer now. I liked the way her voice made me feel.

I was Vale McKinley. I knew that, too. So why didn't I know where I was or what was happening?

"Jonathon, go call the boys," my mother said. Jonathon was my dad and the boys were my brothers. There were four of them. Dylan, Michea, Jonah, and Knox. Why was she calling them?

"Mom," I said finally, and my throat felt raw as I said the words.

"Shhh, don't talk just yet," she said as she looked down at me with tears in her eyes. I noticed her face was thinner, with dark circles under her eyes. Was she sick?

I started to ask, when two women and a man moved my mother

out of the way and began working around me. Talking to me and calling me by name. It took me a moment to realize they were nurses. Turning my head, I finally noticed my surroundings and realized this was a hospital.

Why am I here?

The screeching of tires and my own scream suddenly replayed in my ears, and I saw the terror on Crawford's face before everything went black. Then I remembered nothing. *Crawford.* Where was Crawford? I had to find him. He was hurt.

"She's trying to get up," a nurse said, as another one put her hands on me and eased me back down. "Not so fast. You can't move just yet."

"Crawford," I said in a raspy whisper, and began struggling against them to get free. I had to find Crawford.

The nurses holding me down were talking gently to me in words I wasn't listening to. Where was my mom? I had to get to Crawford. The truck was coming straight at us. I remembered that. He had been so scared.

"Honey, sweetheart, please." Mom's voice was there again, leaning over me, and her hand was on my forehead as she caressed me in what I knew was her calming manner.

"Crawford," I said again.

She glanced up at the nurses.

"The doctor is on the way," one nurse assured my mother.

What did the doctor have to do with this? I had been asleep. I was awake now and I needed to see Crawford. I knew he was hurt.

"He needs to hurry," my mother said, sounding upset. She looked so sick. Why was she here with me when she needed to be in bed?

"Mom," I said.

"Baby, please don't try to talk yet. Just wait on the doctor."

"The boys are on their way." My father's voice, then he was there over me, too. "Hey, baby girl. It's about time you woke up. I've been missing you something fierce."

Those words made my eyes tear up and I wasn't sure if that was because I missed him, too, or because I was scared. Scared of what I was about to find out. Scared of what I didn't know.

"Daddy," I said, and he bent down and pressed a kiss to my forehead.

"You're okay. God took care of you and you're gonna be okay." He said the words like he was reassuring himself and not me.

"Crawford," I said, and like my mother had done, he lifted his eyes to look toward her, then the nurses.

"Sleeping Beauty is awake," a new, deep voice said, and both my parents took a step back. I wanted them near me. They were all I knew. All I remembered.

"She's asking about Crawford," my mother said, and he nodded with a smile.

"She has her memory. That's something to be thankful for. Does she know who she is?"

"Yes, and she knows us," my father said.

"She's been asking about Crawford and trying to talk," the blond nurse added.

The doctor was a young man with red hair and kind eyes. I felt at ease with him, but I wanted answers . . . and if someone didn't give them to me I was getting up out of this bed. I moved my legs and watched as they both shifted under the covers. That was good.

The doctor looked over at the machines I was hooked up to, then back at me. "I'm Dr. Haufman, but so is my father, so I prefer to just go by Dr. Charlie with clients I've been working with for an extended period of time. And you would qualify as such. Now let's check some of that memory. Do you remember your phone number?" Dr. Charlie asked. Why would he ask me something like that? It wasn't important.

But as I started to speak, I realized I didn't know it. But I knew my address. So I told him that instead.

"She's going to have some gaps in her memory. That's normal, but it appears she knows the big things."

I pushed up with both my arms again and looked at my mother. "Where is Crawford?" I asked, my voice getting more strength.

"Get her some ice and a little water to sip on," the doctor told a nurse. Then he glanced back at me. "This is Nurse Everly. She and Nurse Mae have been your two most frequent nurses over the past month. You'll be seeing a lot of them."

Nurse Everly had long blond hair pulled back into a ponytail. She reminded me of a Barbie doll. I wanted to ask about Crawford again.

My throat was so dry.

"It's best that she know everything now. She remembers," the doctor said, then looked at me.

"Sip on some water. You've had tubes in your throat until last night when you began moving and moaning. We have been expecting you to awaken. Your throat will be raw for a while. Taking small sips of water through a straw will help ease it. If you feel like it later, we will send up some ice cream."

This was not the answer I was wanting. *Wait . . . tubes?*

"Why tubes?" I asked.

The doctor walked around and sat down on the edge of the bed like he was an old friend there for a chat. "You've been in a coma, Vale. For one month and three days. You were in a car accident that I think you might remember," he said, pausing for me to respond.

The redheaded nurse handed me a plastic cup of ice water with a straw. I took a sip. I needed it to help me talk. The cold liquid shocked my throat, but eased the pain some. I took a few more sips. Then I put the cup down.

"Crawford. The truck wasn't stopping," I said, thinking about the truck that looked like it had lost control, barreling straight at us. It had come over on our side of the two-way road, and I remembered Crawford jerking the wheel so that the truck would hit him, not me, or the front of the car. But just his side. Then he'd looked at me, and the terror in his eyes was all I remembered.

"The truck you remember was because of a truck driver who had fallen asleep. The truck was coming at you, and Crawford turned the car to the right. In doing so, he saved your life."

"We'll call him. He's fine. He just visited a few days ago. Right now, though, you need to calm down, baby."

He visited a few days ago? That sounded odd. Not like Crawford at all. Where was he?

"I called Crawford." Knox's voice filled the room. "He's at practice. I left him a message."

Practice? I was confused. Practice where? For what?

Mom nodded as if that made sense, and she ran her hand over my head to soothe me. "It's so good to see your eyes."

Knox came up beside her. "Hey," he said simply, and his eyes were instantly filled with tears.

"Hey," I repeated, now worried about him. I had never seen Knox cry. Not even when he broke his collarbone in middle school.

"About time you woke up. First year of college starts soon. Can't have you missing that. Not after all the planning and preparing you've done for it."

College. I was going to college. I tried to remember more, but my head began to pound and I winced.

"Looks like that's enough stimulation for now," Dr. Charlie said.

"Let's give her some quiet time to adjust and rest. The other family will be in here soon, I assume."

Mom nodded but didn't move from my side. "Is it safe for her to close her eyes so soon?" She sounded panicked.

"Yes. She's awake now. The coma is over."

Those words replayed in my head as I drifted off to sleep.

CHAPTER THIRTY-FOUR

VALE

THE NEXT TIME my eyes opened, my room was full. Dylan, my oldest brother, stood by the window looking out. Michea, the next oldest, was sitting on the edge of my bed with a remote control in his hand, watching TV. Jonah, who was supposed to be on active duty in the military, was here standing with his arms crossed over his chest, also watching TV. Knox was staring at his phone as he sat on the sofa beside my dad.

It was my mother who saw my eyes were open and stood from her chair to come to me. "Hey, honey," she said gently.

Her face was so thin it worried me. She seemed to have aged ten years since my graduation. I wanted to ask her about it, but then I remembered.

"There she is," Dylan said, walking over to stand on the other side of me. "You went back to sleep before I could get here and see those baby-blue eyes." His hand covered mine and squeezed. He had dark circles under his eyes, too. I took in the room and the people I loved in it and saw tired faces. They had suffered. Because of me.

"How are the girls?" I asked, my throat raw again.

My mother reached down and pressed a button to sit me up

more before bringing the ice water back to my mouth without my even asking.

"Both Maddy and Malyn miss you terribly. They know you're awake, and they may drive Catherine crazy until we bring them here. I just didn't think you were ready for all that excitement just yet."

I wanted to see my nieces. And my sister-in-law, Catherine. "Tell her to bring them."

Dylan nodded and bent down to kiss my head. "Never been so happy to see you awake in my life. Scared us, little girl."

I managed to smile.

"Stop hogging her. Hell, I've been gone for six months. It's my turn," Jonah said, moving our older brother out of the way. The last time I had seen Jonah was Christmas, when he got to come home for two nights. His buzzed haircut was so hard to get used to. He'd always had a head full growing up. Wearing it to his shoulders most of the time.

"I missed you," I told him.

His eyes seemed glassy, like he had unshed tears, and my heart hurt for him. For all of them. If one of them had been in the hospital, I would have felt the same way. We were all so close.

"Missed you, too," he said as he squeezed my hand.

"Turns out they give you an excused leave when your baby sister is in a coma."

Coma. That word seemed so foreign, yet familiar. I'd been in a coma.

"When was the wreck?" I asked.

Jonah looked up at our mother, who still stood on my other side.

"The night of graduation." Her voice was soft.

I remembered that. "So it's July now?" I asked.

"Not yet. June twenty-eighth," my mother replied.

"Summer has sucked without you," Knox said as he sat down on the end of my bed. "I come home for summer break, and you sleep through the whole first half."

I smiled. That was Knox. Always trying to make a joke. He was the comedian of the family.

"I'm not sure that was funny," Michea said, sounding concerned. Michea was the protector.

"It was," I assured him, and Knox winked at me.

"Let's get her some ice cream," my father suggested, and Michea immediately offered to go get it.

"*Grey's Anatomy* is on. Kind of appropriate. You up for an episode?" Knox asked, sitting back on the sofa as the show began.

I wasn't sure. I felt lost. Like someone was missing, or I was missing. A life I thought I had was gone. Which I didn't completely understand. But my family needed me to be okay. I would be okay for them. The stress and worry this had caused them was evident on all their faces. I was awake. I had survived. I owed it to them to be okay. Even if inside I wasn't okay.

"Sure," I agreed. My mother instantly smiled and I needed to see that. Her face hadn't been smiling lately. The frown and worry lines were proof she hadn't been well the past month. I needed to do this for her especially.

"I'm going to go get Catherine and the girls. They'll want to be here for the ice cream," Dylan announced.

"Okay . . . be careful," my father called out, and I saw Dylan frown then nod before stepping out of the room. I wasn't sure I'd heard Dad say *be careful* over something as simple as going to pick someone up. Many things had changed.

Not just my life but also theirs. Our family had never dealt with this kind of fear. It had shaken us, and yet here we all were. The life of summertime sun tea, ice pops, neighborhood barbecues, and sneaking cookies from Momma's big strawberry jar were the easy happy memories we all had. No real pain.

Until now.

Laying my head back, I closed my eyes. I heard Meredith Grey on the TV and Jonah telling Dad about the new place he was going next. But all I could do was breathe. Because I'd woken up to a life I wasn't sure of. Crawford still wasn't here. And then . . . there was someone else missing. Someone important. I just didn't know who.

"She's sleeping. Turn that down." Michea's voice returned. He was back with the ice cream, but I'd wait on the girls to eat it. I just wanted a moment to hide behind my closed eyes. This would be my only escape for a while. I didn't imagine they were going to leave me alone anytime soon. And I wasn't sure I wanted them to. The demons in the darkness now were lurking. The memories and the terror of that night would never leave me.

CHAPTER THIRTY-FIVE

SLATE

"FULL HOUSE, MOTHERFUCKER," Uncle D said, slapping his cards down on the rolling tray table that sat between me and him.

The old man was as foul-mouthed as he was good at Texas Hold 'Em. I knew playing a game with him would give him bragging rights for the next week, but I did it anyway. He had just survived yet another surgery to remove the tumors in his body, only to find out he was eaten up. There was no way of getting it all. He'd have to go through chemo and then maybe that would give him a few extra months. But right now he wasn't accepting that.

"I need a Coke. You want something?" I asked him, standing up.

"Giving up?" he asked in a mocking tone.

"Hell no. Just thirsty. Thought I'd check in on Knox and his sister. Haven't seen him today." I had run into my fraternity brother a week after his sister had been admitted to the hospital. It was before Uncle D's surgery. His little sister was in a coma from a car accident. He had been so damn pale and looked like he hadn't slept in weeks. I'd been trying to stop by and bring him a coffee every morning. Today, though, Uncle D's doctor had stopped me in the hall to give me the news that he didn't expect Uncle D to live six months with chemo. Or maybe a month without.

Uncle D was saying he didn't want the chemo. I wasn't ready to lose him. He was all I had. I was arguing with him and his stubborn ass.

"Poor family. Tell the boy not to be a stranger." He shook his head. "Take your time, but get me a goddamn coffee and a smoke."

We were in a hospital. He knew he wasn't getting a smoke. Yet here he was still asking for it. "I'll be back with coffee," I told him pointedly. "You want the remote?" I asked, handing it to him.

"Yeah, I'll watch me some trash TV. Better than the real shit."

Smiling, I walked out of his room. That man had been the one to show up and take me from the system after my mother was found dead. The state would have thrown me from one foster home to another if he hadn't come and taken me in. I'd worked hard for him, and he'd taught me to be a man.

Knox was walking down the hallway toward the elevator when I stepped into the hall leading to his sister's room. I was welcomed there. His family was always offering me food and asking about my uncle. They were the good kind of people I wasn't used to being around. Seeing his sister hooked up to machines and unresponsive had been heartbreaking. She was so young and beautiful. I knew the color of her eyes, even though she'd never opened them. I had seen photos. In photos she was always laughing or smiling. There was something warm and real about her that made you want to be near that. It was obvious her family thought the same thing. Knox was close to her. I understood worrying about losing someone you loved. I was dealing with the same thing.

"HEY, MAN, HOW'S it going?" I asked Knox once I was close enough. He smiled. A real smile. One I hadn't seen since the end-of-the-year party we'd had at Kappa Sigma.

"She's awake," he said. "And she's okay. Talking, remembers everything." As he said that, a frown replaced his smile. "Asking about Crawford, and I haven't been able to get his ass on the phone. He's enjoying the college life a little too much."

I'd gotten bad news today, but hearing Knox's news helped. Uncle D would be happy to hear she was awake. He'd been worrying about her since I told him the girl was a frat brother's sister. He was a grumpy old man, but he had a huge heart.

"That's great news. I was about to get you some coffee and check in with you. I'm glad to hear she's awake. I know the rest of the family is relieved."

"Yeah. I don't know how much longer my momma could have gone. Vale is her baby—hell, she's all our baby. It was killing Momma, though. She's dropped about fifteen pounds and she was a tiny woman to start with."

"Anything I can do for y'all? Can I get Vale something?" I needed to help. It was weird because Knox and I were friends, but we weren't that tight. Until this past month at the hospital. Spending time with his family helped me deal with Uncle D's cancer. Seeing Vale lying there always got to me. I felt like we had a connection, as weird as that sounded. I thought maybe it was because her accident happened about the same time Uncle D collapsed in a coughing fit and a pool of blood at the barn the day I got home from school. Uncle D knew about the tumors on his lungs. He just hadn't told me yet.

"Thanks. We're good right now. Michea is getting her ice cream and she's resting. Tell your uncle I'll be by later to get whipped in Texas Hold 'Em."

Knox had visited us at least three times a week over the past month. He would bring food his mother had made and always played Uncle D in a game of poker. Uncle D liked Knox. It had made his sister's story more real to him. Knowing the boy whose family was keeping vigil by the girl's bed. Waiting. I was looking forward to telling him she was awake.

"I'll tell him. He just beat my ass. I decided I needed a breather before I came back and he gloated the next few hours."

"Hey, Slate." A curvy blond nurse I think was named Hope winked and blew me a kiss as she walked by. I'd fucked her in the linen closet three days ago. The stress was getting to me, and she'd been pressing her tits out and licking her lips. I'd decided to go focus on a hot fuck. It had helped for a little while.

I nodded, not sure if I was right with the name. "Hey."

Knox chuckled. "Seriously? You nailed that one, didn't you?"

I shrugged. She wasn't the first nurse here I'd nailed.

I wasn't proud of it. I was just used to it. Been easy to get laid since I was fifteen years old. Especially older women. Maria Grace had been eighteen with seriously huge tits the day I lost my virginity to her under the football bleachers. I'd been a freshman and she'd been a senior. Good times.

Maria was on her second kid and still unmarried last I heard. Shame she didn't go on to college. But she was pretty successful dancing on a pole. I'd seen her show two years ago at Murphy's Titty Bar.

"How much longer y'all gonna be here?" he asked me.

I shrugged. "Uncle D isn't agreeing to chemo. So, not sure. Maybe a few days, maybe a week."

Knox looked truly worried for me and Uncle D. "If I can do anything, let me know."

"Will do. Thanks. And same goes. Y'all need someone to go

run and get something, just tell me. I always need a break from the old man."

We said our good-byes and I watched him go before staring down the hall toward his sister's room. I was really glad she'd woken up. That she was going to be okay. I was also curious about her. I felt like I knew her now, and I'd never even met her. I knew her face so clearly. I'd watched her sleeping. I had read to her. Talked about Uncle D. Given the family a break many evenings while they went home to bathe or sleep. She had become important to me. But I didn't even know the sound of her voice.

I really wanted to.

CHAPTER THIRTY-SIX

VALE

IT WAS THE third day since I had woken up when Crawford walked into the room. He was carrying a dozen red roses, and in the center, one daisy. I had been watching TV, but my mind wasn't on the show or the things my mother randomly chattered on about.

"Crawford," my mother said, sounding delighted.

I stared at him and he did the same with me. We didn't speak. I wasn't going to say anything until he did. I'd woken up from a coma three days ago. Where had he been? At football practice? Bington was only an hour's drive away.

"Hey," he said as I sat still and unblinking.

I remained silent.

Mom stood up and made an excuse to leave the room and give us some time. I didn't respond to her. The words *take him with you* were on the tip of my tongue.

"I'm sorry I wasn't here when you woke up. Everyone thought you'd want me to go on to practice. If I didn't show up for practice, I'd lose my scholarship. I had to make a decision, Vale."

Again. He had three days to find time to get here to see me. "I understand why you went and why you weren't here when I woke up."

He could read between the lines. He was a smart guy. Always had been. I didn't need to spell it out for him.

He put the flowers in the silver vase by the bedside table and reached for my hand. "I stayed here at first. I didn't leave. But my parents and your family insisted it was unhealthy and that you wouldn't want me to do that."

Surprisingly, he still didn't get it. Maybe he'd had too many licks to the head so far in college football. I hadn't been expecting to feel so hard toward him. This was new. Since I had woken up and realized he wasn't here, I hadn't been angry. Just unattached. I couldn't explain it. Somehow I had just accepted things had changed, and no tears or heartache came with that.

"I understand why you weren't here," I repeated.

He frowned and ran his thumb over my hand. "You aren't happy to see me now."

"It's been three days," I finally said. He wasn't going to get it otherwise.

He sighed and nodded. "I know. I didn't get Knox's message until yesterday. We practice all day and I crash at night. I hadn't had my phone even charged until last night."

Yet his girlfriend was in a coma. He hadn't charged his phone. Still he saw nothing odd about this. Maybe he had always been this way and I had just accepted it. During my time in the coma it seemed I had changed. Not him. Me.

"I see" was my response.

Before, I would have kissed him and held him close and said I was so happy to see him. I would have asked about football and all he had been doing. I would have done and said whatever I needed to make him smile. Now . . . I just didn't care.

"You're hurt," he said, looking upset. "God, Vale, I am so sorry.

I swear if I hadn't been so damn exhausted from practice every day I would have thought about the fact I needed to keep my phone charged. I should have been here as soon as you opened your eyes. I'll never forgive myself for that."

He seemed sincere. But the tug at my heart he used to control wasn't there anymore. Was it because I had been asleep for so long? I wasn't sure what had happened.

The door opened and Nurse Mae walked in. "I see you have more company. But it's time for your rehab. Get those muscles moving. I'm excited to see what you can do today since you surprised us all yesterday with your determination."

I had pushed until I couldn't push anymore yesterday. I wanted out of here and I wanted my life back. Or, possibly, a different life back. "I'm ready. He was just leaving," I replied, glancing back at Crawford.

"Thanks for coming to see me. Good luck with football," I said, and he winced. It had been cold. I knew that, but I didn't have any warmth for him.

"I'm going to wait here. I don't want to leave you."

I didn't want to come back here after the grueling workout they would put me through and deal with more of this. "No. I'd rather you not. I'll see you next time."

He looked defeated. There was a small part of me that felt guilty about that. The look on his face and the way my words were affecting him. I wasn't sure if it was from the habit I had of trying to make him happy, or if I should truly feel guilty about how I was treating him.

I reminded myself that he had taken three days to get here to see me. *Three.* Even his best guy friend had stopped by to check on me before he had. That had spoken volumes.

"I'll be back tomorrow," he promised.

"Okay" was all I said. Not sure I believed him.

He left the room after one long look at me for more than an okay.

Once he was gone I turned back to Mae, who had become a friend—if a nurse could become a friend. She was kind and liked to make me laugh with her jokes. I preferred her over the other nurse, Everly. I had actually requested only Mae take me to rehabilitation every day. On Mae's days off, another nurse named Sam came in to help.

"Let me guess. Crawford," she said, raising her eyebrows.

I nodded. "Yep."

"Does he realize he's a little late?"

I shrugged. "Yeah, but I don't think I can care enough to really say anything more about it to him. Before, he was my world. But now . . . he isn't. There are more important things for me to focus on."

She nodded in agreement. "Like kicking ass today in the gym."

I laughed. Mae made me do that often. "Yes, like kicking ass today in the gym."

CHAPTER THIRTY-SEVEN

SLATE

THE TWO-STORY BRICK home was bigger than what I'd grown up in, but not that much. I expected it to be a lot larger than this. They did have five kids. Seemed like that would require more house.

I stepped up onto the porch, still unsure if this was a good idea. Knox had called and invited me to dinner. Said his mom wanted to cook for me and send a plate home to Uncle D. I wasn't good with the big family setting simply because I'd never been around it.

If I was being completely honest, I would admit I was here because of the girl and my curiosity. I wanted to see her awake. Hear her talk. Watch her with her family. We'd both gone through a life-changing event at the same time. Maybe that was what drew me to her, or maybe I was just a nosy son of a bitch. Whatever the reason, I was here. Because of her.

She had surprised even the doctors by her will to conquer rehab. They had released her after only a week. She had to come back once a week to the rehabilitation clinic, but other than that she had been sent home to live her life.

I had been on my way to her room when Everly, a nurse I really wish I hadn't fucked this summer, told me she had been released. Then she'd invited me over for the night. The woman was at least five years older than me and I wasn't convinced she wasn't married. There was something secretive about her.

I lifted my hand to knock when the door swung open and Knox stood there with a grin. "You made it."

"Yep," I replied. "Not going to miss out on home-cooked food."

"I hear ya. I have to ride home to Momma's some weekends because I miss the eating. The fast food and cafeteria food get old during the week."

It was all I knew, but I nodded like I understood the difference. Uncle D and I had lived on microwave dinners. The one time he tried to cook spaghetti, he set the stove on fire and we ended up at the burger joint in town.

"Lucky for you the whole family won't be here tonight. Momma has been keeping the crowd back for Vale's sake. She's adjusting to being home and all."

I was glad to hear I didn't have to do the big family thing. I was curious about Vale, not the other brothers.

"How's she doing?" I asked, following Knox inside.

He shrugged. "Good, I guess. She's quiet. Less chatty and lively than she once was. But the doctors said that's normal. She'll be back to herself soon."

In the photos I'd seen of her before, she was always laughing and smiling. That smile and the way her eyes danced were two of the things that drew me in. Made me want to know more about her.

"I don't think so. Here, Momma, let me do it." A female voice caught my ears and I paused. It was her. Even without having heard the voice before, I knew it was hers. It may be simply because she was the only girl I knew to be here, but still. The sound of her voice fit the face I'd seen.

"Okay, fine. You butter the bread. I'll worry about mixing up the tea," Mrs. McKinley said.

"Come on in here and meet my sister." Knox led me into the bright white-and-yellow kitchen. "Company is here," he announced.

My gaze went directly to hers. Her dark hair was different—washed and full of body. It hung long down her back, curling at the ends. She and Knox had the same clear blue eyes. Almost like you could see through them. I'd never admired Knox's before, but on his sister they had a different effect.

"Mom, you know Slate," Knox said.

I turned my attention to his mother. "Hello, Mrs. McKinley. Thanks for having me."

She waved a hand at me. "Now, I've told you to just call me Karen. We're past the proper 'Mrs. McKinley.' We've had pound cake and coffee together too many times for that." Her smile was genuine. I had always felt like she wanted me around when I'd come by Vale's hospital room.

"Yes, ma'am," I replied with a smile.

Knox stepped toward his sister and I was able to focus on her again.

"And this, as you know, is Vale. Vale, my frat brother Slate. Although he spent plenty of time in your hospital room reading to you, you've never actually met."

Her smile wasn't real. Her eyes looked too lost to truly smile. But she tried.

"It's nice to meet you," she said, moving toward me to greet me with a handshake, which I thought was cute. It didn't last long, though. Her tiny hand was gone too soon and she then gave the attention back to the bread she was buttering.

"We're almost ready to eat. Your dad is out back messing with that old engine in the lawn mower again. I swear that man is too stubborn for his own good. We need to just buy a new one, for goodness's sake."

Knox nodded. "So I need to go get him. Is that what you're saying?"

"Yes, you run and get him and have him wash up. Slate, why don't you have a seat anywhere you like around the table and I'll bring you a fresh glass of sweet tea. I want to hear how your uncle is doing."

Knox patted me on the back. "Sorry, bro, she's nosy. It comes with the food," he whispered, then headed to the back door of the kitchen.

"Uncle D is playing hardball. Won't take the chemo treatments and they're talking about sending him home next week. But I know he'll be smoking a pack a day once we get there and that's no good."

I glanced over at Vale and she was watching me. Listening. There was concern in her eyes and I knew it was for my uncle. Something about that got to me. A girl who had just woken up from a coma to find out she had missed a month of her life, caring about someone else's problems. Most girls I knew were too shallow.

"What happens if he doesn't have the chemo?" Vale asked. She had a really good voice. The sadness in her eyes was hard to look at. It bothered me. A girl like her should be protected. Not have to face hard shit.

"He'll die sooner. The chemo won't cure him. Just prolong his life."

She sighed and put her knife down. "I don't know that I blame him. Chemo sounds like a terrible thing. But for you, I'm very sorry. I wouldn't want my parents to go earlier than they had to, either."

The frankness of her words was refreshing. She didn't try to make it sound better. I needed that.

"Could you get him to stop smoking when he goes home? Might help things," Karen said. That was the kind of suggestion I was used to.

"I don't expect that would be fair, Momma. He's a sick man and he is dying. Why take away something he enjoys? Would that really help at this point?" Again, Vale's words were exactly what I was thinking. She got it. She made me feel more human. Stating my thoughts as if they made sense.

Karen nodded and let out a sigh. "I suppose you're right."

Vale didn't respond. Instead she put the bread in the oven, then washed the butter from her hands and dried them. I watched her every move. She was fascinating. This girl who I had thought about so often over the past few weeks. Even before she woke up.

CHAPTER THIRTY-EIGHT

VALE

IT WAS HARD not to watch Slate Allen during dinner. He was beautiful, but there was something more there. Something I didn't understand, but I wanted to. It was like I knew him. He had read to me while I was in my coma. Which I understood was because he was friends with Knox and up at the hospital visiting his uncle. He was just being nice.

I wanted to do something nice for him. Momma had sent food to Slate and his uncle over the past weeks. But I felt like I owed them both a thank-you. For Slate taking time to give my family a break while sitting with me, and for his uncle giving up the time he had with Slate for me. I just wasn't sure yet what that might be.

"I think I've convinced Mom and Dad to let Vale go to school next month. I promised to bring her home once a week for rehab until they release her. But she's kicking ass right now—" Knox was cut off by the clearing of Momma's throat.

"Language, please," she said, frowning at him.

Knox just chuckled. "Sure. Sorry." He cut his eyes to Slate and grinned. I was sure they both talked a lot worse than that at college. This year Knox would move in to the frat house. I wondered if Slate lived there, too.

"Are you ready to go?" Slate asked, and I felt his gaze locked on me.

I was. And I wasn't. Before, it had been mine and Crawford's dream. Now it was just mine. He had come back to the hospital the next day and we had managed to talk some about school and my plans. He kept telling me he missed me and wanted to be near me.

I softened to him some, but I still wasn't the girl I had been. I wasn't going back to her, either. She had lost herself. And I had found her again.

"I'm already enrolled and my first semester is paid for, so I would hate to miss that. Plus there's no reason for me to stay here." That was the best answer I had. Because the truth was, Bington was really Crawford's choice. Not mine.

"It sounds like you're not sure," Slate said, studying me. He didn't seem to care that my brother and mother were in the room listening to us. It was like it was just us and no one else was there.

"I'm nervous. Unsure, I guess."

"You'll be fine. I'm there," Knox said, patting me on the back for reassurance.

I knew that, but I still was having nightmares. Of the wreck. Those last seconds before everything went black. My family wasn't talking about it, but they knew. Mom had slept in my room last night to wake me when they started.

The doorbell rang and Mom stood up, placing the napkin in her lap to the right of her plate. "Not sure who that could be," she said to herself more than anyone else. "Excuse me. I'll be right back."

"What day are you planning on moving?" Slate asked me. He seemed curious about my decisions and future. That was odd, but the way he looked at me—as if he could see something there important—I wanted to answer him.

"Not sure. We didn't talk about that. Just that I would be going."

Before anyone else could say more, Mom returned . . . and with her was Crawford. He glanced at Knox with a nod, then at Slate. He didn't seem very interested in who Slate was, and his attention moved directly to me.

"Seems we have another dinner guest," Mom said, motioning for Crawford to sit down across from me.

"No, ma'am. I've already eaten, but thank you. I just wanted to speak with Vale a minute if that's okay."

"Of course," Mom replied, and I felt like pointing out I was in the middle of eating, but I didn't want to be rude. So I stood up and motioned my head toward the door to the kitchen.

"This way," I directed, and realized again how I had just made a decision. I hadn't allowed Crawford to determine where we would talk. I didn't wait on him but went on outside and let him follow.

When we were far enough from the door that our voices wouldn't be overheard, I stopped and turned to look at him.

"I came back after practice. It feels different between us, and I want to fix it, Vale. I just don't know how to."

I wasn't sure it was fixable. But Crawford was a big part of my past. He had been in my life for the majority of it, and I loved him. I just felt different about him since opening my eyes—and it wasn't because he hadn't been there.

"I'm not sure, either" was my honest response.

He sighed and ran a hand through his hair. "I love you, Vale."

And I loved him. But it was different. I didn't know how to explain it. So instead of trying, I said, "I know."

He closed the distance between us and placed a hand on my arm before leaning in to kiss me. It was nice. Safe. Everything I knew . . . yet it was missing something. The kiss was no different from any other he'd given me . . . maybe a bit sweeter, more gentle. But it was empty. Like I'd tasted a deeper kind and wanted it again. But I knew he'd been the only boy I had ever kissed. There had been no one else.

I kissed him back, hoping to fill the void, but even when the kiss ended and he smiled down at me like he always had, I felt a little lost.

That night I dreamed of more. Heat, breathtaking excitement, and a rush like I had never experienced. It was the *more* that filled me. I wasn't lost but happy. And it wasn't Crawford who was making me feel that way. The boy from my childhood, the boy I could trust above all others, never once entered that dream. It was almost as if he didn't exist.

In that world for a moment it was just me and . . . Slate Allen.

CHAPTER THIRTY-NINE
SLATE

DROPPING MY BAGS in my room, I looked around the frat house. I'd be sharing a room with Knox this year. I got to choose my roommate, and he was the easy choice. We had gotten closer this summer than I'd ever been to another guy. Both of us dealing with our own pain in the hospital.

Knox wasn't here yet, though. He had texted that he'd be helping his sister get moved in to her dorm first. His parents were nervous about leaving her, even though she had been making excellent progress. Knox said she would only require physical therapy every other week for another month.

I hadn't seen Vale again since that night at her house when her boyfriend showed up and took her away for the rest of the evening. I asked about her, though. Knox always said she was adjusting and doing better. He never gave me more information than that. And honestly, why the hell did I need it? I was worried about her because she was my friend's sister. That was what I was going to tell myself until I fucking believed it.

Oddly enough, my uncle asked about her regularly, too. It was as if the two of us had some weird fascination with this girl. He'd mention often she was a special kind, and that was even off the wall for him. How would he know? He'd only heard about her and seen her on the news.

"Hey, Slate," a female voice purred from behind me. Katie, a blonde from one of the sororities nearby, stood smiling at my door.

"Katie," I replied, not in the mood for this.

Katie had been after me all last year. She had slept with three of my friends. I wasn't going there. I knew how clingy she got and I didn't want to deal with a crazy.

"How was your summer?" she asked, sauntering into the room in a pair of shorts that didn't cover her ass cheeks.

"My uncle is dying of cancer. Spent most of it in a hospital." I decided the honest, direct approach would run her off easy enough.

As expected, she paused and frowned like she had no idea how to respond to that. She was dressed to fuck. Not to discuss my dying uncle. "Oh, um, I'm sorry to hear that."

Yeah, I bet she was. I turned to open my bag and started unpacking.

"Well, if you need anything, you know where you can reach me."

Yes, I did. But I wouldn't be reaching her. "Yeah," I replied.

She made an excuse, said good-bye, and left. I didn't even glance back. That would have been too much encouragement.

When the door clicked shut behind her, I dropped the shirt in my hand and sank down onto my bed. Silence. Alone. I needed this. Soon there would be very little time to myself. The frat house was never quiet or peaceful. There was rarely time to just sit and think. Actually, never time to just sit and think.

Last year I'd loved that. The constant party and the girls. Now I had other things on my mind. Being so far away from Uncle D wasn't easy. I worried about him. I couldn't get there fast enough if I needed to. That was the hardest part. He wasn't taking the chemo, but he'd lived almost two months since they said he wouldn't live even one without it. He was weak and he was hurting. The pain medicine helped ease it, but it wasn't enough. He wouldn't take enough to completely kill the pain, because then he was unconscious and he wanted to be awake. He wanted to enjoy his life.

I'd tried to stay home this semester. To be with him. But he'd adamantly refused. He wanted me here. He said he needed to leave this world knowing I was getting my degree and achieving more in life than he had. Although I thought his life was something to be proud of, he saw it differently. He wanted more for me.

Being here felt wrong, though. Like I was leaving him when he needed me most. It was hard to do. Explaining that to the stubborn old man had been impossible. He was set that I would go to college this semester.

The door opened, and I sat up, prepared for another girl. But it was Knox. "She had eight boxes of shit, three suitcases, and then my parents to drive me nuts. But she's here and I'm thankful for that."

I didn't need more explanation for that statement. I knew he was talking about Vale. "She all moved in?" I asked.

"Oh yeah. She's all moved in. Rooming with another freshman who seems as nervous as she is. I'm just glad she didn't get some raging bitch. My first year I was in a room with a psycho who had these little board game figurines on a shelf by his bed that he talked to at night. That shit was fucked."

He threw his bag onto his bed and sat down.

"Hopefully her roommate doesn't talk to game pieces," I replied, glad to have something else to think about other than Uncle D.

"I don't think my parents will ever leave, though. They're hovering over her. Like she might break. If she comes running here to hide, I won't be surprised."

The idea of her running here was appealing to me. Which I needed to check. I was not going to think about that girl all the time.

"Duke and Neil are sharing a room. I saw it on my way up. Did you know that? They'll kill each other," Knox said, laughing.

"Whose idea was that?" I asked, thinking two more opposite people could not exist.

"I have no idea. But that should be some funny shit."

I agreed. It would be entertaining to watch. And to listen to. If Duke wasn't such a big teddy bear, he'd toss Neil and his OCD ways out the window. Though he might do it anyway. Definitely not going to be a dull moment around here this year.

"I need to unpack and go see if Vale will get something to eat with me. Mom's afraid she'll hide out in her room and not go anywhere. Want to come?"

Yes. I stopped myself before I said it, though. If Knox thought I was interested in his sister in any way, he'd blow up on me. We were friends, but he knew me too well to accept me as being anywhere good enough for his sister. I saw that. I was aware of it, but damned if I didn't want to be around her.

"Sure. I could eat." That sounded less excited and more like me.

He pulled his phone out of his pocket. "Let me text her so she doesn't crawl in bed and hide before then."

CHAPTER FORTY

VALE

MY ROOMMATE'S NAME was Jude. I'd never heard of a girl called Jude, but I thought that was cool. Very unique. She was also incredibly shy. I was okay with that. I would definitely get quiet time, and for that, I considered myself lucky.

When my parents finally left, my brother texted that he was taking me to dinner. He didn't ask. He told me. I would rather unpack my room and read a book, but I agreed to go. I would unpack tomorrow. Jude was busy unpacking her many, many stuffed animals and placing them on her bed.

She had a soft blue bunny in her hands that she was being more gentle with than the others. My curiosity and the silence in the room got the best of me, so I decided to ask.

"You collect those?"

She stopped debating where to put the bunny and turned to look at me. She had big brown eyes and a chubby face with freckles. Her dark blond hair was cut short and she looked younger than a college freshman. But who was I to judge? Maybe I did, too.

"Not exactly," she said in a soft voice. I wondered if she ever talked louder.

I gave her a moment to respond, wondering if "not exactly" was all the answer I was going to get.

Finally, as I was about to ask more, she put the blue bunny on her bed and picked up a very old yellow bear and showed me. "This was the first one. My birth mother sent it to me on my first birthday. Then every year after, she sent me a stuffed animal on my birthday. My mom said it was my birth mother's way of letting me know she thought of me and was glad I had a good home. So I kept them with me at night. To remind me I had two mothers who cared about me and that was . . . special."

I had not been expecting that explanation.

"That's beautiful," I replied honestly.

She smiled then, and her face was really pretty when she smiled. "It is, isn't it?"

I was going to like Jude.

"How old were you when you were adopted?" I asked, without wondering if that was appropriate to ask.

"My parents brought me home from the hospital after I was born. My birth mother was only fifteen. She wasn't ready to raise a child."

I had gone to high school with a fifteen-year-old mom. It had been hard on her. I remember her coming in to school late, looking exhausted, after the baby was born. She had late nights with her newborn and still managed to get to school that first year. By the time the baby was a year old, though, she had dropped out and ended up getting her GED. I couldn't really blame her.

"Where are you from?" I asked.

"Oklahoma City," she said. "A long way from home."

I was only a little over an hour away. I couldn't imagine being that far from my parents. "Yeah, it is."

She sighed and pulled out one more stuffed animal from the box. It was a pink elephant that she placed in front. "That's my newest one," she said. "My birthday was last week."

I wanted to know if she had ever met her birth mother, but I figured I'd pried enough at this point. So I didn't ask any more. "All eighteen of them," I replied with a smile.

"Guess I should unpack some," I said, standing up and going for a box. I still had an hour before Knox would be picking me up for dinner.

"There are two shelves in the bathroom. Which one do you want?" Jude asked.

I shrugged. "You go ahead and unpack. I'll take whatever you don't use. I'm not picky."

"Okay. I'll take the higher shelf since I'm taller, if that's okay."

"Sounds perfect."

Things in this part of my new life were going to be easy enough. I just wasn't sure about the rest of it.

KNOX TEXTED ME that he was outside a little over an hour later, so I told Jude good-bye and grabbed my purse to go down and meet him. What he hadn't told me was that he was bringing a friend.

I stepped outside and smiled at Slate Allen. I hadn't seen him since the night he came to our house to eat. My dream about him that night hadn't been the only one. I had dreamed of him several nights a week since then. The dreams were vivid . . . and sometimes explicit. I hadn't wanted to face him.

However, I did think about him and his uncle a lot. He had read to me when I was in my coma, and I wanted to do something for him. So I'd visited his uncle twice. Mom had made him some pound cake once, and another time she sent him meat loaf. She made the best meat loaf. I liked his uncle, who insisted that I call him Uncle D. He had known exactly who I was and seemed happy for me to visit. I just wish I'd been able to go visit him again before he was sent back home to Huntsville.

"Hello, Slate. It's nice to see you again," I said, sounding a little too proper, but I didn't know what else to say. I had dreamed of him with a lot less clothing on and I was afraid my cheeks would heat.

"You settling in okay?" he asked.

I nodded. "Yes, thank you. I hear you're stuck with him all year," I said, nudging my brother as we began to walk out to his truck. Anything to make this seem less awkward. It was only so for me, though. I was the one having wild naughty dreams about him.

"Or he's stuck with me," Slate replied.

"More like I'm stuck with him," Knox said, making Slate chuckle.

I wasn't going to ask about their frat house life. Some things a sister did not need to know.

"How's your uncle?" I asked Slate, changing the subject to something I was actually concerned about.

"Hanging in there. He's in pain, though," Slate said.

"Tell him hello for me. Or maybe you could give me his mailing address and I could send him a letter. I had hoped I'd get by to see him at least one more time before he went back home. I had promised him some of Momma's apple pie my next visit."

Glancing over at Slate, I noticed he had a confused frown on his face. Was I not supposed to tell him I took his uncle food?

"You visited Uncle D?" he asked, slowing down.

I had assumed his uncle would have told him. I hoped I wasn't telling him something Uncle D didn't want him to know. "Yes," I finally replied with caution.

Knox began to laugh, and Slate looked at him, then back at me.

"The sneaky bastard. That's where the lemon pound cake came from."

Knox continued to laugh.

"I took him some pound cake that Momma sent and went to visit him two days after the dinner you came to. You'd mentioned him and I figured he could use some company and something good to eat. I hope that's okay."

I wasn't sure why it wouldn't be okay. Slate had read to me and brought my family coffee and muffins often. I appreciated him doing that and wanted to do something in return.

CHAPTER FORTY-ONE
SLATE

THE OLD MAN had spent time with Vale. No wonder he was so curious about her and concerned about how she was doing. But he didn't tell me. I wasn't sure why he wanted to keep that a secret, but I'd call him out on it at the next visit. Might even take him a lemon pound cake to do it.

"I'm sure you made his day with your visits. He just didn't tell me about them, so I was surprised. Guess he wanted to keep you to himself."

Vale smiled at that comment, and damn, that smile was something else. Her eyes lit up when her smile was real. It was hard to look away from her when she was like that.

"I'll be going up to visit him next weekend. You're always welcome to come along." I said the words before thinking about them. Her smile made my brain short out, apparently.

"I'd like that. I could go by my parents' and get him that apple pie."

Knox wasn't laughing anymore, and I knew why. I really should have thought before I spoke. "You could come, too, Knox," I added.

He shot me a look that made it obvious he was thinking about my intentions. He wasn't so sure about me at the moment. But my uncle was dying, so I could tell he was trying to keep an open mind.

"I might do that," he finally replied.

When we got to his truck, I was relieved. I had made the conversation awkward all because her smile got to me. Also the fact she'd been visiting Uncle D and because she truly worried about the old man. Had nothing to do with getting near me. Her blond nurse, Everly, had started acting like she cared about Uncle D and showing up in his room only when I was there, to flirt with me. I saw through that shit easy enough. It had gotten to the point I tried not to visit Knox and his family when Everly was on duty. Her flirting was obvious and annoying.

I didn't like her using my sick uncle to get to me.

Vale was different.

And she was not my speed. She was good and kind. I had to let this fascination with her go. But first I was taking her to see Uncle D. Because . . . well, because she fucking smiled and made me a little crazy.

"I'll get in the back," Vale said when I opened the passenger side of Knox's truck.

"I'm the tag-along—I'll get in back," I argued.

She shook her head and began climbing in back. Her ass in those jeans was a little more than distracting.

"Nope. I'm smallest and there's not a lot of room back here," she said, then thankfully sat that butt in the seat and out of my face.

"She's stubborn. No reason to argue," Knox told me as he got inside.

"Let's go get some pancakes at the Pancake Haven. We talked

about the place enough this summer. Need to show Vale what all the fuss is about," Knox said.

I agreed. I missed the strawberry and cream pancakes.

"Breakfast for dinner. I like it," Vale said from the backseat.

"I know. You're always the reason Mom pulls out the biscuits and gravy for dinner," Knox told her with affection in his voice.

I'd witnessed him stay in a constant state of fear and worry this summer when she'd been in a coma. He had watched her breathe . . . as though if he stopped watching, she might not take another breath. He said they'd been really close, and he told me stories of their childhood. Things that made him laugh, and it was good to see him smile at those times.

It was almost as if he were the parent at times. I knew just listening to him that Vale McKinley was special. The kind of special that changed a person. That made a mark in life. I didn't like thinking she wouldn't wake up. It was one of the reasons I went to read to her. I would talk to her, too. Tell her why she needed to open her eyes. I talked about college and how much fun she'd have. I did all I could to make her want to live.

"Mom is already texting me," Vale said from the backseat with a soft laugh.

"Surprise. She hasn't texted me," Knox replied.

"She's glad we're going to dinner. She was worried I'd stay in the room and read all night once she found out Crawford had an away practice game."

Knox lifted his gaze and looked at her through the rearview mirror. "That is exactly what you were going to do."

"True . . . but I was going to unpack, too."

"Trust me, the pancakes at this place are worth it. You'll thank me after the first bite."

Knox pulled into the parking lot and groaned. "Shit. Mia is here."

Mia was his girlfriend for about four months last year. Until she decided to start cutting out photos of wedding dresses and shit like that. Knox had bolted. Mia had been the insane ex-girlfriend for a while. Showing up unannounced, crying, bringing him cookies . . . it had been a joke at the frat house by the end of the year.

"The girl from last year?" Vale asked, sounding excited.

Knox sighed. "Yeah."

Vale giggled and clapped her hands as if that were the best news ever. "Oh, this is great. I can't wait to meet her. Next family dinner I can fill everyone in."

"You're a brat and you're not meeting her," Knox said, opening the door to get out.

I got out, then offered a hand for Vale. She slipped her small hand into mine, completely trusting me, and I liked that a hell of a lot.

When she stepped out, she looked up at the restaurant and frowned. It wasn't a fancy place, but I didn't think she was one to care about that.

"Not what you expected?" I asked her.

She glanced at me, then back at the sign. "I don't know why I had an image of this place in my head, but I thought I knew what it looked like. I didn't." She shook her head. "Guess I dreamed it."

"You'll be dreaming about these pancakes," Knox told her, walking around the truck to meet us. "Come on, let's go eat. And do not talk to Mia or make eye contact with her. That goes for both of you."

Vale started laughing and I fucking soaked that shit up. Damn.

CHAPTER FORTY-TWO

VALE

THE TREES WERE full of fall colors, and I stood in the path with my head thrown back, staring up at the blue sky peeking through the branches. It was as if I were in a fairy-tale world out here. Beautiful and perfect. The sound of the stream running through the rocks along with the birds chirping filled the air, and I laughed and spun in a circle with my arms spread wide.

This felt like falling in love. The simple beauty of it. So detailed, yet fluid. The wind blew through my hair and I inhaled the fresh air. Then he said my name and my heart fluttered and pleasure coursed through me. I loved hearing him say my name. He was what made this perfect. Dropping my arms, I turned toward his voice.

And there he stood, so tall. His dark hair brushing his shoulders and his green eyes full of laughter from catching me dancing under the trees. He was my safe place. I hadn't known I was lost until he found me.

Slate Allen was my hero.

MY EYES FLEW open. That was a new one. My feelings for him were stronger in that one. Like I wanted to run and hide in his arms.

Know he wasn't leaving me. This was all crazy, because Slate was not the kind of guy you had these dreams about. Crawford was.

Slate was a player. He liked women, and they liked him. That was obvious at dinner last night. He'd dated most of the females in there, it seemed. Several came over to flirt and rub up against him. Then the way Knox talked about him and his conquests being legendary, you would think my brain would register all that and stop having silly dreams about him.

It must have been something I ate. No one should eat that much whipped cream and chocolate before bedtime. It must have the same effect as pizza. Crazy dreams. I wanted these dreams to stop. Looking at him made it hard when I had these images in my head.

I glanced over at Jude, and she was sleeping soundly. All eighteen stuffed animals in bed with her—it was a packed house. Smiling at the sight she made, I got up to go to the bathroom. It wasn't even six in the morning yet, but I was going to get a shower. I didn't want to close my eyes again. My dreams couldn't be trusted.

I took my time washing my hair and drying it. Dressing was easy enough with the sunlight finally coming into the room. Jude was a hard sleeper and didn't even budge while I got myself ready. I was going to go find coffee and take my book with me. I wasn't sure just how late Jude slept and I didn't want to wake her early.

Deciding against driving, I chose to walk toward the campus center. I needed to find the library, too. That was important. There were several books I was supposed to have on my reading log for two different classes.

No one was awake. The early morning light was something to take in on the quiet campus. I doubted I would walk through it empty like this again. Today was Sunday. On Monday classes would begin. Today the rest of the students would arrive and get settled. It was move-in weekend. I wondered how long it would be before the campus started stirring with activity. I knew Crawford had gotten back late because he'd texted me. I didn't expect to hear from him until closer to lunch.

I passed the main office and turned on the downtown street when the smell of coffee finally met my nose. I was getting close. I saw someone walk out of a storefront up ahead with a coffee in his hand and knew I'd found what I was looking for—and walking distance from the dorm. That was really good news.

In the café window, EARLY PERK was painted in green with brown and yellow accents. There was a display of huge muffins and pastries just under the name, and I decided this might be my new favorite place. Café tables with yellow umbrellas were scattered along the sidewalk out front. Inside there were about seven tables, and benches lined the walls.

I inhaled again as I walked in the door. This was exactly like I expected. Which was odd. Why I expected anything, I wasn't sure. I'd heard my brother talk about his college life plenty last year, and although he wasn't very descriptive, I have a vivid imagination and tended to create how I think things should look in my head. This coffee shop, for example.

My mother had always said I should write books. All my life I've had a very bright and colorful imagination. I liked telling stories and exploring other realities. It was my escape many times to daydream.

The barista was a girl about my age. A job here wouldn't be bad. I'd enjoy being in this atmosphere.

"What can I get you?" she asked with a smile. Her short brown hair was curly and had a wild look to it that I liked. She had a pixie-shaped face that it fit with. An interesting tattoo of tiny birds flying away went down into her neckline.

"I have two questions," I told her.

"Okay."

"Are they hiring here?" I asked her.

Her smile became a relieved one. "Oh my God, yes. We just lost our other weekend girl and I'm here alone until twelve when the afternoon help arrives. No one wants weekend mornings from five to twelve. Then one more day during the week you would have to work a five to twelve."

I had no problem with early mornings. "I don't have morning classes on Thursdays. Would that work?"

The girl actually bounced on her feet. "Yes! Here." She scrambled under the counter in front of her and pulled out a paper and a pen. "Fill this out and I'll call Jane, the owner, while you do that. She might hire you today."

"Great!" I had been worried finding a job was going to be much more difficult than this. I loved this little place. Working here on weekend mornings would be perfect.

I sat down at the nearest table and began filling out the paperwork.

"Hey, what was your other question?" the girl called out. "And I'm Isla, by the way."

"It's nice to meet you, Isla. I'm Vale, and I was going to ask what coffee you suggested. The menu is extensive."

She beamed at me. "Let me fix you up."

I ended up drinking my café mocha latte with whipped cream while she taught me where everything was in the back and how to work the espresso machine.

I had a job.

CHAPTER FORTY-THREE

SLATE

THE FIRST WEEK of classes always sucked. Getting all the paper-work and syllabuses stressed me the hell out. Then add the fact Uncle D had passed out Wednesday and busted his head open while hospice was there; his being sent back to the hospital just made it worse. I had been told hospice would take care of him. That shit shouldn't have happened.

It was hard to concentrate on anything when my thoughts were with Uncle D. I called him a couple times a day and it was annoying the hell out of him. He sounded so damn weak, though. Even more so than when I had seen him last.

Once I got to my room on Thursday after my morning classes, I dropped my books and all the damn paperwork they'd given us on my bed and let out a frustrated growl. I shouldn't be here. I should be with my uncle. This was bullshit. He shouldn't expect me to stay here while he was fucking dying.

The scholarship I was on wouldn't let me drop out this semes-ter to go spend it with him. But I was at the point where I just didn't care. I'd get a school loan when I needed to return.

Convincing Uncle D of this was going to be hard, though.

A knock on my door interrupted my thoughts. *I swear to God, if it's a girl I may lose my shit.* I hadn't dated since I got back here and I wasn't in the mind-set for anything. I was terrified every time my phone rang that it was a call about my uncle. I didn't have time for dating drama.

"Yeah," I barked unwelcomingly. Just in case it wasn't a brother.

The door opened slowly, like the person on the other side wasn't sure it was a good idea to come in. "What do you want?" I asked again, ready to get this over with.

Then Vale appeared and all my frustration evaporated. That was not who I was expecting. She wasn't here for me, of course, but seeing her after days of making myself not look for her on campus was nice. It felt good when nothing else in my life felt good.

Knox would fucking kill me if he could read my thoughts.

"I'm . . . I'm sorry if this is a bad time. . . ." She sounded nervous, and I realized I'd all but bit her head off for knocking.

"No, no, I thought you were someone else. Come in. I'm just going over all this first-of-the-semester shit they drown us in."

She nodded. "Yeah, it's a lot."

She was still nervous.

"Knox isn't here." I stated the obvious.

"Yeah, I know. I talked to him. I actually stopped by to see you. I would have called, but I don't have your number and I didn't want to ask Knox because he'd assume . . ." She trailed off and blushed. The pink on her cheeks was damn adorable.

"I don't mind you stopping by whenever you want," I told her honestly.

"Thanks. I just . . . I know we talked about me going with you to see your uncle this weekend and I really want to, but I wasn't sure when you were going. See, I got a job at Early Perk and I work five to twelve every weekend morning. I'd ask off, but I just got the job and this will be my first weekend. I'm afraid I might lose my job if I do."

I hated that she was so nervous with me. Her cheeks were still pink, and she could barely look me in the eyes. I wanted her comfortable with me. Simply so I could listen to her talk and look at those amazing eyes of hers.

"Yeah, no, you don't need to ask off and lose that. It's a great place. I'm glad you found a job so fast. Uncle D is actually back at the hospital in Franklin. We could leave around one on Saturday and stay the afternoon with him. Maybe eat dinner with him, then head back here around eight."

She was frowning. That concerned look she got. "What happened? Did hospice send him back?"

"He fell with a hospice worker there. Apparently he got up in the middle of the night because he's stubborn. Hit his head and they had to send him back due to blood loss."

Her frown deepened. "Oh no. That's terrible. Bless his heart. This has got to be so hard on you, being here. Yes, if you don't mind waiting on me, I would love to go Saturday. But if you want to go on early, I can drive up after work. I know my way to Franklin."

I was selfish. I wanted to see Uncle D, but I wanted her with me. "I'll wait on you. Be better driving back late. Your brother would feel better about me driving."

She nodded. "Yes, I'm sure he would. But if you need to get there, I am perfectly capable of driving at night. He likes to pretend I'm still eight years old with pigtails, but I'm not."

No, she definitely was not.

"I'll wait on you," I repeated.

She sighed and nodded. "Okay. I'll bring coffee and muffins. Mom will have us an apple pie ready."

I wish my uncle could actually eat an apple pie. He was on an IV and refusing to eat. When he tried, he threw it up.

"Thanks. But he's not keeping food down. Doubt he'll be able to enjoy that pie."

Her eyes looked so full of sadness and sorrow I wanted to hug her. Not to make her feel better, but because she could feel that for an old man she hardly knew. Uncle D didn't have many people in his life. We'd worked on the farm and he hadn't been a social man. Having someone care about him like that other than me meant so damn much.

"Then I'll be sure to have some entertaining stories to tell him. He likes my stories," she said with a nod. Like that was her mission now. If she only knew how just showing up would be enough for him and for me.

"I'm sure he'll love that."

She smiled. A sad one. Then turned to leave. I was watching her go, unsure what to say and wondering about Crawford. Where was he? Did he not care about her going with me to Franklin?

CHAPTER FORTY-FOUR

VALE

WHEN I GOT back to my room, Jude was sitting on the bed with a book in her hands, and the smell of daisies hit me. I glanced over to see a huge bouquet by my bed. Crawford.

"Your boyfriend stopped by," she said, smiling. "He's really nice."

Yes, he was. Always nice. The perfect guy.

I hadn't turned my phone on all morning, so I wasn't sure if he had texted or called. I knew he had practice again today. That and his classes. I didn't see a reason to bother him. But seeing the flowers made me feel guilty.

He was busy here and I had let him be. I didn't go out of my way to see him. During classes yesterday, I had seen a glimpse of him surrounded by girls. He seemed to be enjoying himself. And the odd thing was, I didn't care.

That bothered me the most.

I took the card from the flowers and opened it up.

This week has been too busy and I miss you. Sunday afternoon is ours. I have somewhere I want to take you. Love, Crawford

I didn't read it again. Instead, I sat the card down on the table and looked straight ahead out the window. I'd never felt so lost.

SATURDAY MORNING I arrived thirty minutes early to help Isla get the place open. I had worked with Connie and Blake on Thursday morning. Isla worked on Wednesday mornings and weekends.

Isla was a lot more pleasant than Connie. I was almost convinced that Connie hated the job. Blake was a lot more chipper, and I enjoyed chatting with him during down times. Connie texted a lot and mumbled curse words. Not real pleasant.

Blake was a senior at Bington and was majoring in mass communications. I had been considering that and was curious if he was happy with that decision now that he was almost done.

I did pick up on the fact Blake wasn't a fan of the Greek, so I didn't mention my brother being in Kappa Sigma. I myself wasn't going to join a sorority simply because I liked to keep to myself. I wasn't a very social person.

When things started to pick up on Saturday, it was almost nine. Even then, the early crowd was over thirty. The college-age crowd didn't start drifting in until closer to ten. I had almost learned how to make all the drinks without the cheat sheet taped to the counter. I also knew all the different muffins now and the names of the pastries.

"God, he is gorgeous," Isla said under her breath as she handed me a chocolate-chip muffin. I started to ask who, when I followed her gaze to see Slate walking in the door.

Oh.

"He's a slut, though. Sleeps with a girl, then on to the next one the next day. I wouldn't go there, but I love to look at him. He's got a pirate thing going for him. He just needs an earring," she added with a giggle.

Slate's eyes met mine and I smiled. This was going to be a hard day for him. Isla didn't know that. She only knew what Slate had let the world around him see. I knew he had a reputation, but he was also a human. Someone's nephew. He had a soul. And it was hurting.

I handed a customer his muffin. I wasn't sure how to respond to Isla or if I should just let her estimation of him go. Maybe that was what he wanted people to think. Who was I to change that?

"Can I help you?" I asked the next customer.

"A Butterfinger latte with light whip and a banana nut muffin. Two forks, and make it warm, please."

I rang them up before going to fix the drink. This was a popular one. I made it several times a day. Isla came with the large muffin, nice and warm, on a plate with two forks. We made a good team in the mornings.

"Here you go," I told the customer.

Then Slate stepped up. "Good morning," I said, knowing this wasn't a good morning for him.

He smiled at me and the sadness seemed to fade. I had an urge to hug him. I'd had that Thursday in his room, too. It had taken all my willpower not to.

"Morning. You look good in the yellow apron," he replied. His voice still had the raspy, sleepy sound to it. He hadn't been awake long.

I held it out and curtsied, because somehow I knew he would laugh. It was weird how I sometimes could anticipate what he needed from me. Like I expected him to, he laughed. A real one.

"Now, what can I get you?"

"Black coffee and one of those cream-cheese croissant things."

"Chocolate or vanilla?"

"Vanilla."

I nodded. "Good choice. I don't like the chocolate one."

"Me either."

I turned to see Isla watching me like I had lost my mind. I was confused for a moment, then remembered what she had said when he walked in. Normally she was off getting the customers' food request. Not this time. She was frozen in her spot. It was awkward, so I smiled at her and said, "Isla, this is my friend Slate. Slate, this is Isla. She's the pro here and is teaching me everything."

Slate nodded her way and smiled. "Nice to meet you, Isla."

"Uh, yeah, uh, you too," she said, then cut her eyes at me like she couldn't believe me before going to get his croissant.

I fixed his black coffee. The easiest drink I had done all day.

"You enjoying the job?" Slate asked as I handed him his coffee.

I nodded. "Yes. It's fun, and I get to smell coffee all morning. It doesn't get much better."

He chuckled just as Isla came back with his croissant. He thanked her and I was afraid she'd melt in a puddle on the floor. She barely got out a "you're welcome" before running to the back room.

"You have a reputation around these parts," I teased, knowing he'd understand exactly what I was talking about.

He smirked. "Your talking to me and calling me your 'friend' is going to confuse the hell out of everyone. I don't have female friends."

I would have laughed. I should have smiled. But those words. I knew them. They were so familiar. Which made no sense. My chest tightened when he said them, like I . . . like I missed them.

"You okay?" His voice snapped me out of the weird in-between state I had drifted into.

"Yeah, I'm good. Bit of a headache," I lied.

"I'll go grab you some Tylenol."

I shook my head. "No, it's okay. I just need coffee, and luckily I can fix that easy enough."

He didn't seem convinced. But he finally took his things and went to find a table. One where I could see him and he could see me. Something about that also made me feel like I had done this before. Was I dreaming about him and not remembering it?

"Why didn't you shut me up and tell me he was your friend when I was talking about him?" Isla whispered behind me.

I turned to look at her. "I know his reputation. I didn't have time to explain he is my brother's frat brother and roommate. We met this summer."

That was the most I was willing to tell her right now. My coma and Slate being in my hospital room while I wasn't awake was more information than she needed.

CHAPTER FORTY-FIVE

SLATE

THE DRIVE TO Franklin would have been so hard without Vale. I was worried. No, I was terrified of what I'd see. Of how Uncle D would look. The little boy in me wasn't ready to see him at death's door. Barely hanging on. I needed him. I wasn't ready to let him go.

Vale's voice, her ability to keep my mind off things, and the way she shifted in her seat and crossed and uncrossed her legs was enough to keep me preoccupied.

However, when we finally pulled in to the parking deck of the hospital, all my fears came to meet me head-on. I paused after we were parked for a minute to mentally coach myself for what I was about to see. I loved that man in the hospital room, and I hated seeing him in pain.

Vale leaned over and placed her hand on mine. "I wish I could tell you this won't be hard. It will be. It's going to hurt and your heart will ache. But he needs to see you smile. He needs to hear you laugh. He needs to know you'll be okay."

She was right. These weren't empty words of encouragement. She was being real. I had to face this and be exactly what that man in there needed me to be. When I'd been without parents, he had stepped in and been what I needed, and that couldn't have been easy. But he did it. He'd sacrificed for me my entire life.

I owed him everything.

"Thanks," I said, looking at her. Those pretty blue eyes were wet with unshed tears.

"Let's go make a memory" was what she said, but what we both knew she meant was *"This may be the last time. Let's make it count."*

I nodded and we got out of my Jeep.

The walk inside had been one I'd done every day for almost a month. During that time, she'd been sleeping. Missing life. Would my time with my uncle this summer have been easier with her? Somehow I thought it would have been. She made things easier. Just being there. Just being her.

When we stepped out of the elevator, Everly was walking out of a room and stopped to look at the both of us. She gave a fake smile that didn't match the expression in her eyes.

"I see after all his visiting you this summer, you've made friends now you're awake," she said, not sounding at all happy about it. Everly was that kind of woman. The one that wanted to be the prettiest, the most desired. Unfortunately, she wanted it so badly it was unattractive. Those were the worst kind. Her hotness factor was seriously hit by her selfishness.

Vale paused and studied her a moment, then she smiled as if remembering. "Oh, you were one of my nurses. That time after I woke up is still a little blurry for me. I'm working through what was real and what wasn't."

Everly gave another fake smile and pointed down the hall. "Your uncle is in two forty-six."

"Thanks," I said, touching Vale's elbow to turn her in the right direction, and moved us on down the hallway. Far away from Everly. My sleeping with some of the nurses this summer must have gotten around. She was more than likely bitter about that.

"I don't think she's very nice," Vale said, as if she was turning it over in her head.

I laughed. "No, she's not."

"Shame. She's so pretty."

That kind of honesty was the kind that attracted men. And Vale didn't have one damn clue.

We reached my uncle's door and I stopped, unable to open it. As mentally prepared as I tried to make myself, the thought of walking into that room and seeing him even more frail wasn't easy.

Vale reached for my hand and squeezed it, then opened the door because she realized I wasn't going to be able to.

We walked inside slowly and my eyes landed on him. He was asleep. Hooked up to monitors and machines. An oxygen mask covered his nose and mouth. He looked as if he'd lost twenty pounds in a week.

My stomach clenched and my chest hurt so badly I needed to sit down. If this was real fear, I'd never truly experienced it until now. Even when they'd told me my mother was dead, I hadn't been this scared. As a child, I didn't think about facing life alone.

Vale let my hand go and walked over to stand beside Uncle D's bed. I did the best I could to move closer.

"I've come to visit, just like I promised I would. You better open those eyes for me." Her tone was soft and teasing.

Uncle D blinked and finally focused on Vale looking down at him. A smile touched his thin, dry lips.

"Look who's here," he rasped.

She beamed at him. "I am without apple pie, I'm afraid, but I did bring something else. I think it's better than apple pie, personally," she said, then looked over at me.

Uncle D turned his head and his eyes met mine. They were never very expressive eyes, but as pale as they were now I could see love in them. I'd never questioned his love for me, even though we didn't say that word much around our house. Our actions spoke clearly enough.

"I guess that'll do," he said. His words were so soft, you had to strain to hear him.

It had only been a week since I'd seen him last, and yet he seemed months different. Like half the man he was just last Saturday.

"I leave you for a week, old man, and this happens," I said, finally closing the distance between us.

He gave a weak laugh.

"Why didn't you tell me Vale had visited you before? Had to hear it from her," I said, wanting to reach down to hold his hand in mine but not doing it. We weren't affectionate like that.

"Keeping her to myself," he replied, and this time I laughed.

"You just wanted my momma's good cooking," Vale said, and he turned his eyes toward her.

"That, too," he agreed.

There would be no Texas Hold 'Em today. He barely had any energy to talk. The idea that there would never again be a hand of Texas Hold 'Em between us bit deep.

"You know I told you I wasn't sure about college. But I did go, and I'm glad I did. You were right. I couldn't sit back and let life go on without me," she said to my uncle.

His smile grew, but his eyes seemed heavy.

"Good girl," he replied.

She lifted her gaze to mine as if noticing the same thing.

"Rest your eyes, Uncle D. We're gonna get comfortable and hang out here. We will be waiting to talk more when you wake up," I told him.

He nodded and his eyes closed. But as they did, he reached his hand out to mine and patted it gently.

I was glad his eyes were closed when the tears I was fighting back finally broke free and rolled down my face.

CHAPTER FORTY-SIX

VALE

UNCLE D DIDN'T open his eyes again that day. I called my mother to come get me and drive me back to campus. Slate couldn't leave. I didn't want to abandon him there, but I intended to come back after work tomorrow. I'd have to explain to Crawford, but I couldn't let Slate deal with this alone. He had looked so lost when I left. I asked Mom to take him something to eat and visit with him tomorrow until I could get back.

She had promised she would.

Later that night my phone rang, and I quickly answered it.

"It's Slate." His voice was hoarse and I gripped the phone tightly. Afraid of why he was calling. "I hope I didn't wake you. I just needed to talk."

The panic eased, and I went into the bathroom so I wouldn't disturb Jude as she slept.

"I was awake," I assured him.

"Your mom came by late with a slice of chocolate cake and a big glass of milk. It was nice." I hadn't known she was taking him anything tonight. But I was thankful she had.

"Good. Has he opened his eyes?" I asked, afraid to hear the answer.

"No," he replied. "Doctor says he doubts he will again."

I wanted to be there. I wanted to hug him. I hated him being alone right now. If Knox hadn't started his job at the bar in town, he'd have gone with us today. But he had to work evenings.

"I should be there by two tomorrow at the latest," I said.

"Thank you. It's hard being alone. Watching him breathe. Wondering if he's hurting or just resting. I want him to go peacefully. What if I hadn't gotten here when I did? What if he'd closed his eyes and I didn't get to see him one more time?"

"He was waiting on you, Slate. He was fighting it because he was waiting on you. Seeing you was what he needed. That pat on your hand was his way of telling you he loved you."

I heard him inhale deeply. I hadn't meant to upset him. Just reassure him. "I should have told him I loved him," he said.

"He knew. Your actions were enough."

"He should have gotten the words," Slate argued.

Sometimes we don't get that. "You didn't know it was the last time you'd get to speak to him. He's resting now because he knows you are there and he is loved."

He was quiet for a moment. Then I could hear him move around. "Thanks, I needed to hear that."

"You're welcome," I replied.

"And, Vale?" he said.

"Yes?"

He paused, then sighed. "Never mind. I'll see you tomorrow."

THE NEXT MORNING, work was hard to get through because my mind was somewhere else. Worrying about Slate and how he was handling things. My mother texted me when she arrived at the hospital to let me know she was with him. That helped. But I still wanted to be there.

I had called Crawford the day before to explain what was going on, but he hadn't answered his phone. It was the last Saturday before game season began, and I knew he had practiced hard all day. I typed out a text explaining it and told him to call after twelve. I was working this morning. Again, something else we hadn't talked about. I wasn't even sure he knew about my job. The last two times we chatted he told me all about what he was doing but didn't actually ask about me.

The more I thought about it, the more I realized it had always been that way. Crawford liked to talk about himself, and I had liked to listen. I never wanted attention or the spotlight and I knew he did. It had been okay then. But since waking up, that bothered me. Along with so many other things.

Isla asked me several times at work if I was okay. She noticed my mood and I liked that about her. She paid attention and cared. I explained a friend's uncle was dying. I needed to leave as soon as I could to get to the hospital. It was slow by eleven, so she told me to go on.

When I pulled up to the hospital, my phone rang and it was Crawford. I parked and answered.

"Hey," I said.

"Hey, so you got a job?"

"Yeah. I need to work and help my parents with my costs, like Knox does." He hadn't asked about Slate's uncle first. I found that odd. It was the bigger issue.

"I just woke up an hour ago. I was going to come get you for brunch, but I got your text. So, you know this Slate guy that well? I thought he was Knox's friend."

The touch of jealousy in his tone didn't go unnoticed. I almost mentioned the herd of women surrounding him this week but didn't. It was pointless and I didn't have the time or energy for the argument that would start.

"He read to me when I was in a coma. Gave my family a break regularly and brought them coffee and muffins. That makes him my friend, too. Even if our friendship started while I was asleep."

He was silent for a moment. I let him think about what I'd said, and hopefully he'd have a reasonable response.

"You know his reputation, don't you? I mean, you don't want to be heaped in the pile with those girls. People will assume that's what you are."

I gripped the phone a little too tightly in my hand. I couldn't blow up on him. That wasn't fair. He had his concerns and I needed to let him have them. But I wasn't bending to his will. Those days were over.

"He is my friend. He needs a friend right now. I don't care who says what. I know the truth and that's all that matters. Do you have a problem with that?" My tone had gotten snappy and I could tell he was startled by it.

"Uh, no. I guess I don't."

"Good. Mom's in there with him now. I need to go. I'll text you when I'm headed back." I almost added that we could get together but didn't. Because I wasn't sure I'd be in the mood to see him. Not after what I was about to face.

Ending the call the way we had for years, we said, "I love you," but this time it felt different. Like I didn't truly mean it. I shoved those thoughts from my head and made my way inside.

My mom sat in a chair beside the window and Slate sat beside his uncle. He had one of Uncle D's hands in his. When I stepped inside, his head turned to me and I saw gratitude and relief. My mom was there, but it was me he needed.

"Hey," I said, walking over to him. "How's he been?"

Slate sighed. "The same." He glanced over at my mother, who was watching us. "Your mom has been great. I just wish I had more of an appetite to eat the food she brought. What I could eat was really good."

"There's more where that came from. You just eat when you can," she said gently.

"Thank you," Slate told her.

"Mom, you go on. I'll stay until tonight."

She stood up and walked over to Slate. With a squeeze from her hand on his shoulder she said, "Your uncle is a lucky man. He is loved by you and he knows it."

Slate nodded, but he didn't say anything. I could tell he was having a hard time with her words. He swallowed hard.

"Call me if you need anything. I'll bring some dinner over later."

"Thanks, Momma."

She hugged me, then left us there. Watching his uncle hold on, but barely.

"He's bleeding internally from the fall. Nothing they can do, though," he said when the door closed behind my mother. "They don't think he'll make it through the night."

"I'll stay with you." There was no way I could leave him.

"You have classes in the morning," he argued, but it was weak. He wanted me here. He was afraid.

"I'll get what I miss from someone else in my classes."

He didn't try to talk me out of it. Which was good because I wasn't going anywhere.

"I'll have a farm to think about. Not sure how I'm going to

handle that. Uncle D owned all of it. Worked his whole life to own it in full. He told me this summer when he got sick that he'd left everything to me. It was my decision what I did with it. I can't run a farm right now, but I can't just sell it. It was his life."

There were going to be a lot of decisions like this for him to make. Things that wouldn't be easy. I knew they were all starting to run through his mind.

"Does the farm support itself financially?" I asked him.

He nodded.

"Well, why don't you find someone to run it—live there, take care of things, and pay them? When and if the time comes that you want to live there, it will be waiting."

Again, he nodded. "Okay. Yeah, I think in town there'll be some folks who would want to do that."

"Don't stress and worry over things like this just yet. It will work out."

He didn't respond and I figured he needed a moment. I walked over and sat in the seat my mother had deserted. I could smell her homemade doughnuts in the box beside me.

"I've never had someone in my life who would do this," he said, looking over at me. "Stay when things were tough. No one I could trust other than Uncle D."

That made my heart hurt. I had a big family. I had been blessed with so much in life and I'd taken that for granted, while Slate had no one else.

"You have my family now. Me and Knox. We're your friends. With us comes our family."

A sad smile touched Slate's lips and his gaze shifted to the doughnuts. "Yeah, you've got a great family. Not sure what I did to get their support."

I knew what he had done.

"I think it all started with the coffee and muffins you brought to them when they were watching me sleep, wondering if I'd ever wake up. And the reading to me when they needed a break. Kindness like that isn't forgotten."

He shrugged. "Knox was my friend and . . ." He paused and his eyes locked on mine. "And I wanted to see your eyes. I wanted to hear your voice. I wanted to know you. Sleeping Beauty."

Oh.

Oh.

I blinked several times and my face heated.

He chuckled and the sound was nice in the quiet sadness of the room. "You were exactly like I imagined, too. Maybe even better."

I didn't know what to say to that. So I reached for the doughnuts and took one out, then held the box toward him.

"Doughnut?" I asked.

Then he really laughed. And my heart did a silly flutter in my chest.

CHAPTER FORTY-SEVEN

SLATE

AT TWO FIFTY-FIVE that morning, my uncle took his last breath. I was watching his chest rise and fall . . . and then it didn't anymore. I stood up, numb, and although I knew it was coming, I still couldn't believe that he was gone. The only thing I felt was Vale's arms as they came around me and she held me. She was so small, but her little body was comfort. She stayed like that when the nurses came in and pronounced his death and the time. She didn't let go when they covered him and rolled him from the room.

When we had to get his belongings and leave the room, she stayed close to my side. Her parents and her older brother Dylan were in the hall when we walked out. It was like I had a family. People there that I never expected.

Uncle D must have known I'd have this. This was why he liked Vale so much. He could go and know I'd be okay.

Vale slipped her hand in mine as we went out to her car and followed her parents to their house. Her brother Dylan drove my Jeep to the house and then I was offered food I couldn't eat before being shown Knox's bedroom.

When Vale left me there alone, I finally let the tears I'd been battling fall.

The man I had loved since I was a kid was gone. I wouldn't hear him curse anymore, I wouldn't eat burned biscuits and gravy when I came home from school, and he wouldn't beat me at Texas Hold 'Em and brag about it for days. I would miss every one of those things. I'd give anything just to have him back.

Sleep finally came and I was thankful for the darkness.

THE FUNERAL WAS two days later in Huntsville at the small Baptist church my uncle had gone to since he was a boy. His parents had been buried in the graveyard in the back, and so had his wife and child over thirty years ago. She'd died in childbirth, as did their baby girl. He had never remarried or even dated.

He told me once that when you find the woman you can love forever, you don't get over her. I didn't believe him then, but I wondered as I grew older if maybe that was true.

Vale, Knox, their two brothers who lived in Franklin, and their parents were there beside me. The people from town who had known Uncle D and the church folk all stood around his grave as he was lowered into the ground. Vale's hand stayed in mine through it all. It was like she knew I could fall apart if she wasn't there to help me.

Knox stood on the other side of me, and it was like I had a family. I couldn't help but feel like Uncle D had orchestrated this all before he left. I wasn't alone. If he could watch things from up there in the beer-drinking, cursing, poker-playing heaven he was in, he was smiling. This would make him happy.

Especially the roses on his grave with the deck of cards fanned out in a circle as the centerpiece. That had been Vale's idea. He'd think that was a riot.

Knox's hand was on my shoulder as the first shovel of dirt

covered the grave. Uncle D was really gone. But I would live a life that would make him proud of me.

Lifting my head toward the sky, I said a silent thank-you for the life he'd given me. The little boy who needed a home was given not only that, but also the love of an old man who needed someone himself. We had been there for each other and it had worked for both of us. I wouldn't have wanted it any other way.

CHAPTER FORTY-EIGHT

VALE

AFTER THE FUNERAL, Slate decided to stay at the farm a few days and help the older couple he had hired to take care of things get settled in. They'd get to live rent-free and they would earn twenty percent of the profit from Uncle D's beef cattle, pigs, chickens, and vegetable garden.

The town had gotten the word out that Slate was looking for help, and he had takers within days. That had been one worry off his mind. My dad had helped him some, too, until he was able to head back to school.

It was a week later when Slate walked into the coffee shop at eight on a Saturday morning. He smiled at me when our eyes met, and although we had been texting daily, it was good to see him. I'd missed him.

"Hey," I said, wanting to run around the counter to hug him but feeling as if that time was over. Hugging him when his uncle had just passed was okay, but now it seemed . . . different. So I stayed put behind the counter.

"Morning. Just got back and I need a black coffee with a chocolate-chip muffin."

"Coming right up," I said, holding up my hand to stop him from getting out money. "This is on me. A welcome-back breakfast. I can't cook like my momma, but I can buy your coffee and muffin."

"I sure am gonna miss your momma's cooking," he said. "And thank you."

"You can come home with us anytime. And you're welcome."

Isla walked out of the back and paused when she saw Slate. She knew about his uncle now and she wasn't so focused on his man-whore ways. "Hey," she said, blushing as she spoke to him.

"Hello. Isla, isn't it?" he said, smiling at her. I wondered if he was aware of what that smile did to women. Probably.

"Yeah . . . uh, how are you?" she asked, leaning on the counter toward him.

I started to make his coffee and warm his muffin because it didn't look like Isla was going to be helping me.

"Getting by. Thanks," he replied.

"You, or, uh, if you need anything. I'd be happy to help," she said.

This was not the Isla I was used to. For starters, her flirting was normally much better than that. I wanted to laugh, but I didn't. I understood that Slate was gorgeous. It was hard not to notice.

"Uh, thanks," he said awkwardly.

She giggled. She actually *giggled*. "Sure. Anytime."

I warmed the muffin and hurried back to him before she embarrassed herself any more. She was going to replay this over and over all day and slap herself on the forehead for it. And I was going to have to listen to it.

Walking up behind her, I smiled at Slate and handed him his order. He looked as if he was studying me. Looking for something. I wasn't sure what that was, but then he turned back to Isla and his expression changed.

"So, what are you doing tonight?"

What?

"Uh, nothing," she said quickly. "Nothing at all."

What was he doing? Isla's flirting was funny, but apparently he liked it. Was he going to use her like he did the others?

"There's a party at Sigma Kappa. Want to come?"

A party at the frat house? What?

"Yes!" she said almost a little too loudly. "I'd love to!"

"I'll meet you there at seven," he replied, then winked before taking his stuff and walking away.

What the hell had just happened?

"Oh. My. God," she breathed as she turned to look at me. "I guess y'all really are just friends like you said. I wasn't sure I believed you but I do now. *OhmyGod!* I am going out with Slate Allen."

Who was that just now? The guy I had gotten to know wasn't what I'd just witnessed. I had heard of his reputation, but I didn't really believe it. The Slate I knew had a big heart. Had he not seen how nervous Isla was and how innocent her flirting had been?

"You don't look happy about this. Are you mad? Do you like him?"

I was frowning at Slate's retreating form as he headed down the street and out of view. "No. I don't like him. Actually, I don't think I know him." Then I turned and asked the next customer what I could get them.

I was at work. I had a job. I would focus on that. Crawford had already made plans for us this evening. I had been reluctant to go, but I'd said yes.

I didn't know Slate Allen at all. But I did know Crawford. It was safe to trust what you knew. Crawford had been trying hard to be

understanding about Slate and supportive while he called and texted trying to get time with me. The guilt from my behavior since
coming to school now sank in.

My feelings for Slate had gotten confused. Wrapped up in him
needing me and knowing there was a good guy underneath all
that. He would only ever be a friend. That is, if he didn't use Isla. If
he respected her tonight.

Still, my chest ached some. I thought he was different. That
he'd changed. I wanted to be right.

CHAPTER FORTY-NINE

SLATE

WHAT THE FUCK had I been thinking?

I slammed my bag onto the bed and growled in frustration. I had gone to see Vale and invite her to the party tonight. Because I didn't want to party—I wanted to see her. But when I saw her face, I couldn't do it. Knox had told me she had a date with Crawford tonight. I couldn't make her choose one of us. I was terrified it wouldn't be me.

And damn, she'd been so beautiful. Her long dark hair pulled back in a ponytail, smiling at me like she was thrilled to see me. Those blue eyes of hers were happy. She was like that for me, a form of sunshine that I needed. She made me fucking happy.

Then the other girl had flirted with me and Vale hadn't seemed to care. She hadn't been jealous—hell, she'd even smiled about it. And why had I wanted to make her jealous? I didn't like jealous-ass girls. So Vale wasn't upset that her friend was flirting. She actually looked like she was trying not to laugh.

That had pissed me off. Damn stupid fucker that I am, I'd asked Isla out to get a reaction from Vale. It had worked. I'd gotten one. One that was going to eat me alive all damn day and night.

Fuck me. I was a bastard. If Uncle D was watching now, he'd be disgusted and calling me a dumbass.

I had to talk to Vale . . . but what was I supposed to say? *I'm sorry? I did that to make you jealous?* I couldn't say that shit, and I couldn't break this date. I knew Vale well enough to know that she wouldn't forgive me for hurting her friend. That selflessness of hers was one of the reasons she was special.

Unable to help myself, I texted her.

What are you doing?

Then I waited. If she ignored me, I was going to find her. Wasn't sure what I'd say, but I'd fucking grovel if I had to.

Studying.

Of course she was. She'd missed a week's worth of classes for me. And now she was catching up. Like I needed to.

God, I hated myself.

"You ready for tonight?" Knox's voice filled the room and I felt even more guilty. His family had been so damn good to me and I'd gone and hurt the girl they all adored.

"Yep," I said, forcing a smile.

He saw the coffee cup in my hand and grinned. "Already seen Vale, then. I know she was happy to have you back. Girl has worried herself sick over you."

He said it like that was funny. But no one had ever worried themselves sick over me. Uncle D worried about me, but no beautiful female with eyes like the sky had ever given a shit if I was hurting. They wanted to fuck me, but that was where it ended.

"Yeah, I did."

"I thought about inviting her and Crawford tonight, but I wasn't sure how that would go with you. I know y'all have gotten close.

She's around you more than Crawford lately—and honestly, that scared the shit out of me at first. But, watching you with her, I trust you. Vale's hard not to want to move mountains for."

"I invited her friend at the coffee shop," I blurted out.

Knox stilled a moment, then looked at me, confused. "Oh" was all he said.

He didn't need to say more. That simple word was enough.

"I figured it would reassure her I was okay, you know?"

Knox only nodded.

He was concerned. I could see it even though he was trying to hide it.

"You said she was studying?" he asked.

"Yeah. I just texted her."

He headed for the door. "I'll see you later," he called out before he was gone.

Shit.

Damn it all to hell.

He was going to check on her, because he was worried she was upset. Damn, I hated myself.

I DIDN'T SEE Knox again until that night. And when I did, he seemed distant. Which answered my question. Vale was not okay and it was my fault.

Isla was nervous most of the evening until I got her to play pool, then she danced with a few of the guys when they asked and I assured her it was fine. But not once did I leave the crowd with her. I made sure Knox saw that I wasn't getting her alone. That was the last thing on my mind. I was worried about Vale, and as soon as I could call it a night with Isla, I was going to find her.

I just had to make sure Isla had a good time, because if she didn't, I knew Vale would be upset about that, too. When one in the morning rolled around and Isla was drunk and still dancing, I figured I better get her back to her place safely.

I dodged another girl by walking off before she could speak. I'd already been propositioned to do, watch, and experience things that were typically too hot to turn down. Fucking-blow-your-load hot, but not now. Vale had changed everything.

CHAPTER FIFTY
VALE

THE LONG WHITE hallway seemed endless. Like I could never get to where I was going. Where was I going? I was lost. Looking for someone. Crawford. He was missing. That was it. I hadn't seen Crawford. I had to find him. The never-ending stretch of white walls and tile floors smelled of antiseptic and death. I was in a hospital. I'd seen too many of those.

I wanted out. I didn't want to be here. Where was everyone? How had I gotten to be so alone? Who left me behind? Was it Crawford? I had to find him. Someone. I didn't like it here.

The walls felt like they were closing in, and my heart pounded in my chest as panic began to set in. I started to run. I had to get out of this. Find the light. Find the way to him. To where I needed to be.

Then a door opened and he stepped out. His long, dark hair tucked behind his ears and his emerald-green eyes on mine. I inhaled deeply for the first time. My heart slowed and I stopped running. The walls opened back up and I was going to be okay. I wasn't lost now. I wasn't alone.

He was there now. In front of me.

"I thought you might need a decent cup of joe," he said. . . .

My eyes opened and I was once again in my dorm room staring at the ceiling. Although I had never been in a long white hallway, lost with walls closing in, there had been something so real and familiar about that dream. As if Slate had been there before. When I was lost. But that didn't make sense.

I thought you might need a decent cup of joe seemed so real.

I sat up and my phone began to buzz. I reached over and picked it up from the nightstand to see Slate's name lighting up the screen. He was calling me. Why? It was three in the morning.

As hurt as I was, I couldn't ignore him. He might need me.

So I answered.

"I need to talk to you."

"Well, here I am."

"No, face-to-face. Please. I'm just outside."

"Where's Isla? Is she okay?"

"I took her home. She's passed out in her room. She's fine."

I paused. Why did he want to talk at three in the morning? "Are you drunk?"

"No. I didn't drink anything tonight."

"Okay. Let me put on a hoodie."

"Thank you."

I didn't say "you're welcome" as I hung up. If I hadn't just had that dream, I probably wouldn't be going outside to talk to him. Typically I had a little more pride than this.

I eased out of bed and quietly put on the hoodie I had gotten when I was sixteen on a trip to Edinburgh. Then I made sure I had my key to get back in before slipping from the room and down to see Slate.

When I stepped outside into the cool night air, Slate was

waiting on the front steps of the building. He looked tired and his hair was slightly messy, like he'd had a rough evening.

"I'm sorry," he said, before I could say anything.

I was about to ask "for what?" when he continued.

"Asking Isla out. I . . . I'd come in there wanting to see you and I had complete intentions of asking you to the party."

"Oh, so you saw her and decided you'd rather take a date than a friend? I get it."

He shook his head and muttered a curse. When he looked back at me, his eyes were dark. "Is that what we are, Vale? Friends? And you had a date already. I knew that."

He knew I had a date with Crawford . . . *oh*. That might change things. I had gone out with Crawford. We had had dinner and seen a movie. It was a military movie. Not my thing, but I had never gotten to choose the movies. My thoughts had been on Slate all night anyway, no matter how hard I tried not to think about him.

"I don't know" was the most honest reply I could give him.

He ran his hands through his hair and groaned in frustration. "Vale, I can't play games with you. Tonight was a stupid game and it made me miserable. I hated it. I made sure Isla had a good time and got her home safe, but I didn't touch her. I did that because she was your friend and she hadn't asked to be a part of a stupid fucked-up game I was playing. But I wanted to be with you. I always want to be with you. But there's Crawford. The love of your life. I can't compete with that. I want to. But I can't sit back and wait to see who you choose. I need to know now. Am I wasting my time waiting on you?"

Crawford was a huge part of my life. Asking me to cut that off now without giving us time was impossible. I owed Crawford more than that. From the time I was six I had pictured my future with Crawford.

"I can't tell you that. I don't know."

Slate nodded and his intense eyes locked on me. "I didn't think so. But I had to ask. Not sure I can be friends, Vale. I'm going to need my own time. Space. You understand?"

I did. My heart felt like it had been ripped out and thrown on the ground to be trampled, but I understood. He had to live his life while I figured out mine.

"Yes."

Then he left. And as I watched him go, I was afraid I had lost something I would regret the rest of my life.

CHAPTER FIFTY-ONE
VALE

LATER THAT DAY, I sat quietly in Crawford's car while he explained why he was disappointed that I had a weekend job. For starters, I would miss all his games. I hadn't thought about that when I took the job. I just needed money.

He had been going on about the way I pulled away from him for over an hour. He was right. I *was* pulling away, and it wasn't fair to him.

"We used to do everything together," he said in a sulk.

"We used to do whatever you wanted to do." I almost covered my mouth in shock that I'd said something like that to him.

He frowned and stared at me. "What?"

He really didn't see it that way. All these years I had accepted the way things were with Crawford . . . comfortable with the way we were. He made the decisions and I went along with them. Until I woke up in the hospital and he didn't show up for three days, that hadn't dawned on me.

"I needed a good job that didn't interfere with my classes and studying. All I have free is the weekends. So I took the job. I love my job. I didn't realize your games were an issue. You don't see me on game day, anyway, most of the time. Y'all travel. I can't follow the team every Saturday. I can't afford that, or expect my parents to pay for it."

He sighed and shook his head. "You're so different since you woke up."

Seriously? *That* was what he got out of this conversation? That I was different. Not a "Yeah, you're right" or an "I didn't think of that."

"Did you not hear what I just said?" I asked him.

"Sure, but you aren't even considering my feelings."

Oh my God.

"You're right. I *am* different since the coma. I woke up and I felt different. I saw things differently. Maybe it was from the near-death experience, or maybe . . . maybe I dreamed of a different life." I stopped. Where had that last bit come from?

"A different life?" he asked, looking at me, confused.

I paused. I wasn't sure why I'd said that. But somehow it felt right. Like I had been asleep until that coma, and while I was fading, I was imagining the life I actually wanted. Although I remember nothing of that time. My memories were the car accident and then opening my eyes in the room to see my mother.

"Crawford, I'm not sure I can be who I was before. I want an opinion. I want my needs to be as important as yours."

Crawford didn't say anything, but he looked out the window toward the dorm where he had parked.

"I don't want to lose you . . . to lose us," he finally said.

"Then don't."

He finally turned to me again. "You're different. It makes us different."

Again, here we were—back to how I was affecting his life. Our plans had been to go to dinner and then to a party at a frat house where he was pledging. But I just wanted to go back to my room and study.

"Maybe we need time." I wasn't sure what he meant by that, but I nodded and reached for the door handle.

"Maybe we do. You think about what I said, and I'll think about what you said. Let's have some space and decide what it is we both want now and for our future."

He watched my hand on the door as I pushed it open, then he nodded. "Yeah, okay."

He didn't stop me or argue, and I was glad. I wanted to be alone. This wasn't an easy conversation, but it was one that needed to be had. I felt free. Instead of feeling weighed down with guilt, among other things, I was lighter.

Crawford had to accept the me I had become if we had a future.

I LEFT HIM alone. Let him decide. It took him two full days before he texted me. The text he finally sent was:

You're right. I'm sorry.

That wasn't what I had been expecting. Nor did it bring relief. Instead, there was still confusion. My feelings for Crawford had changed so much that I wasn't sure there was a chance for us now. The little girl in me wanted there to be a chance, but the me I had become wasn't sure *comfortable* was what I wanted in life.

There was excitement, and thrills, and not knowing the future. Even though I knew nothing about those things, I wanted them. Deep down inside I was craving them.

But he was sorry. And he wanted a chance. I owed him that. Maybe I owed it to me, too.

I replied.

Okay. What does that mean for us?

The photo I had placed by my bed of the two of us at homecoming last year stared back at me. We had been so sure then. No questions about what came next. I didn't miss that girl. She was lost. She just hadn't known it.

There's a party at a friend's apartment. It's his birthday. Will you go with me tonight?

It was a Tuesday night. I needed to study. But this was Crawford trying, so I said yes.

CHAPTER FIFTY-TWO

VALE

THE ONLY WAY they could be getting away with this was that everyone in the apartment complex was in college. Blaring music and laughter could be heard from outside. We had barely made it out of Crawford's car when people called out his name in greeting. This was the football crowd. I hadn't met any of them yet and I realized that was odd.

It was also my fault. I had been keeping Crawford at a distance and it was time I admitted that. I hadn't tried to get to know him or his life here.

"Hey, Crawford, you promised me a dance," a tall, leggy blonde called out.

He tensed beside me and I almost told him it was okay. Because it was. I didn't feel jealous. A bad sign.

"She's a cheerleader. Just a friend," he said, his attention turned to me.

I shrugged. "Okay."

"Who's the babe?" asked a guy with long hair pulled back in a ponytail and beer in his hand.

We had just made it to the entrance of the building.

"Garth, this is my girlfriend, Vale. Vale, this is Garth."

Garth looked surprised by the word *girlfriend*. I began to wonder if this crowd even knew of my existence.

"You did good, man. And you work fast."

Crawford was tensing again. "Vale and I have been together since we were kids."

Garth's eyebrows shot up. "Wow. Well, all righty then. Let's introduce Vale to the group."

THE INSIDE OF the building just got louder. I noticed most of the doors were open and people were pouring out. I was beginning to think I didn't want to meet the group.

Crawford stopped and introduced me to people as we went. I was shocked when he was handed a beer and he took it. That wasn't Crawford-like at all.

No one seemed to know he had a girlfriend. It was a surprise. Only two girls who had come up to paw at him seemed to know who I was. I wondered if it was because he'd had to tell them he was in a relationship at some point.

The blonde from the parking lot kept looking our way, and when she got a chance, shot me smug grins. I wasn't sure what all that was about, but I had a few ideas. I wasn't that naïve.

Crawford was a hit. Everyone wanted to be near him and they all wanted to talk about football. This was his element. I knew that, but I still felt like I didn't fit.

Was this what growing apart felt like? Could that be all this was? We were going our separate ways and this was how it looked.

"What about that dance?" the blonde asked as she wrapped an arm around Crawford's.

I watched him closely to see if she had a reason to feel so comfortable with him.

He chuckled, but it was forced. "Not happening, Cat, but have you met my girlfriend, Vale?"

That was subtle. I'd give it to him. He was trying to handle this without drama. I just wasn't sure it was possible. Cat looked determined.

"No, just like I was unaware of her until last week," Cat said, her eyes narrowing in my direction as if she wanted me to read between the lines. I was reading just fine.

"Excuse me while I take her off your hands," said Dan, a red-headed guy with a buzz cut I had met earlier, as he scooped his arm around Cat and literally pulled her away with him.

"That wasn't what it looked like," Crawford said. He had never lied to me over the years. So now that he was, I saw it clearly.

"We should probably discuss that later," I told him.

He started to say something else and stopped. I would give him a point for being smart and shutting up. He had lied already. No need to dig further.

As the evening wore on, there appeared to be more girls who seemed to feel close to Crawford. It was becoming more and more obvious how far apart our worlds had grown. There was a lot of talking about things they had all done that I wasn't a part of this summer. They laughed together and the inside jokes didn't seem to stop.

I stayed by his side like I always had until I needed some fresh air from the stench of beer and too many people. Excusing my-self, I headed out while Crawford entertained several of his buddies with some story about another friend I didn't know.

Once outside, the noise wasn't as bad and the warm breeze smelled better than the inside of that apartment. How many times had I gone to parties I didn't enjoy with Crawford over the years? I was just now realizing this wasn't that different. Sure, I knew the inside jokes and the stories so I could at least laugh at those, but I had never felt like I had fit. Being Crawford's girlfriend had just made me accepted.

"So *you're* the coma girl." The snide comment came from behind me and I turned to see Cat walking up to me. Fantastic. Just who I wanted to deal with.

I wasn't responding to that. Stooping to her level wasn't something I was willing to do.

"Crawford sure didn't seem to miss out on a good time while you were sleeping."

I had seen enough tonight to know that already.

"He's going to get bored with this. *You.* All guys who come to college with their high school sweethearts realize there is something more exciting out there. They want to taste all the options."

From the sound of things, Crawford probably had tasted some options. I shrugged. "Guess that could go both ways," I finally responded, surprising myself.

She laughed. "As if. When a girl has a guy like Crawford, they don't let go easily."

Sighing, I turned and looked at her. "What do you want?"

She smirked. "Crawford."

I already knew that. "Then why are you out here bothering me?"

She wasn't the sharpest knife in the drawer, that was for sure. Her frown signaling her confusion told me she had no idea what I meant.

"He fucked me. Three times in one night. Once in a bathroom at a club."

That hit my heart hard. It wasn't jealousy, either. It was . . . it was betrayal. I had been in a coma and he'd been . . . he'd been screwing girls in bathrooms at clubs.

I managed not to look like I'd been hit with a brick in the chest. "That says more about you than him," I replied. Actually, it said a lot about both of them.

"What? That I'm a good fuck?" she asked, laughing.

I stood there a moment deciding if I was even going to respond to this girl before I walked away. My chest had been cracked open and I needed to be alone. Finally, I said, "He's in there now without me. Stop wasting your time out here and go get what it is you so obviously want. Because you're not the only one. He's had girls all over him tonight."

Then I walked away. I knew how to get back to the dorms, and I needed the fresh air and silence the next four miles would give me.

CHAPTER FIFTY-THREE

SLATE

I WAS EITHER dodging her or trying to catch glimpses of her. I never knew what I wanted from one minute to the next. I didn't want to see her with Crawford, but then I didn't want to not see her because I missed her. Why couldn't I make up my mind?

"Can we go back to your place?" Grace asked as she slid her hand between my legs and cupped my dick.

That had been my plan, but seeing the football players crawling all over the Tinderwoods Apartments meant there was a party there tonight and I knew *she* would be there. With Crawford. My mind was on her. Always on her.

"Not tonight," I replied, removing her hand. This wasn't the first time I'd turned down sex lately. It was becoming a habit. I couldn't fuck someone and be thinking about Vale the entire time.

But how the hell was I supposed to get over her?

"Why not?" Grace puckered up and leaned in to start nibbling on my ear. I wanted to be able to mindlessly do it like I had before. Take her back to my place, do what she was begging for, and move on. But something had changed in me and I wasn't able to fix it.

I started to move her off me again when I saw Vale . . . walking . . . in the dark . . . alone. What the hell?

I carelessly shoved Grace off me as I slowed and pulled the Jeep up beside Vale. Jerking the door open, I jumped out and called her name.

She was already looking back at me. Her face was hidden in the shadows.

"What are you doing?" I asked her, closing the distance so I could see her face.

"Walking," she said simply. I wanted to laugh at her obvious answer, but the hurt look in her eyes sliced through me.

"Where's Crawford?" I asked, already imagining ways to beat the shit out of him. What guy lets his girl walk home alone in the dark?

"At a party."

I knew what party. I had passed it a half mile ago. "Is that where you're coming from?"

"Slate," Grace called out. I ignored her. Vale didn't, though. Her eyes went to the girl in my car, then back to me.

"I was just tired and ready to go. You need to get back to your date," she said, and started to walk away. I reached out and grabbed her hand.

"You're not walking all the way back to your dorm. It's not safe. Your fu . . . boyfriend should have thought about that." He was going to think about it once I got my hands on him. That was for damn sure.

"He's not my boyfriend. I don't think he has been for a very long time." She tugged at her hand, but I wasn't letting go. Especially after a comment like that one. If he wasn't her boyfriend, then what the hell happened?

"What happened, Vale?" I asked.

She tensed, then I saw the tears in her eyes as she quickly

looked away from me. "Crawford has been with others . . . since coming here."

Was he a dumbass? He had Vale—why would he want anyone else?

"He's an idiot," I said, squeezing her hand gently.

She sniffed and reached up to wipe her eyes.

"Slate, let's go," Grace called out again. I had forgotten she was even there.

Shit. I glanced back at the Jeep, then at Vale. "I need to take her home, then we can go wherever you want and talk. Or drink. Or break things. Just get in my Jeep, please."

Vale started to shake her head, and I pulled her close to me and whispered in her ear, "I will leave that Jeep right there and walk the entire way back with you if you don't. I'm not letting you out of my sight."

She sighed and finally gave me a nod. "Okay."

I wanted to pull her into my arms and swear to her I'd never let anyone hurt her again. But right now I couldn't. Because she may not choose me. She was heartbroken over the guy she did love. Just because I loved her didn't make it enough for both of us.

"Where is she going?" Grace asked as we walked up to the Jeep together. "I'm not getting in the back. She is."

Vale looked up at me. "Sorry about her" was all I could say.

"I like the back," Vale replied.

I held her hand as she crawled up into the Jeep and took the backseat.

"Again, why is she with us?" Grace asked, her tone getting more annoying by the second.

"She needs a ride," I said as I drove back onto the road and toward the sorority house where Grace lived.

"Are you taking me home?" she asked incredulously.

"Yeah."

She glared back at Vale. "Unbelievable. He's worse than his reputation. I hope you know that. If he'll do this to me, he'll do it to you."

I didn't expect Vale to respond, and I wanted to shut Grace up. Even if she had a reason to be pissed. I didn't have time to worry about that.

"Actually, there's a side of Slate no one sees because he doesn't show them. Or they don't look closely. You went out with him because of his reputation. Maybe you should have tried to see beyond what you thought you knew about him."

My heart slammed against my ribs. Girls didn't talk about me like that. They never had.

"Whatever. You're young and stupid. You'll learn," Grace snapped, turning around in her seat.

"Hopefully sooner than you," Vale shot back.

I laughed. I wasn't able to stop myself. Her response was unexpected.

I pulled up in front of Grace's sorority house and she shoved her door open. "Don't call me," she yelled before slamming the door behind her.

I hadn't been planning on it, but I knew it helped her to say it. What had she wanted from me tonight? To say she screwed me? To say she was one of the many? Why? When had that become such a big thing for girls?

I opened my door and held out my hand to Vale. "Come on and get up front."

She didn't argue, and although there was still sadness in her eyes, she didn't look as broken as she had when I picked her up.

CHAPTER FIFTY-FOUR
VALE

I WAS SORRY about the girl. She had been on a date with Slate and he'd ended it for me. I should have been nicer. She just caught me at a bad time.

"What happened?" Slate asked as we started down the dark road.

"What was going to happen sooner or later. We have grown apart."

"There's more to it than that," he said—and he was right.

I stared out the window of the Jeep and wondered when, exactly, did Crawford pull away? When I was in the coma? How long did it take him to go live his life? Had it been hard on him?

"I think if the situation had been reversed . . . I wouldn't have been able to go so easily or quickly. I was only in a coma for a little over a month. We had been together since we were six. Wouldn't it take longer than a month for him to accept that he needed to go on with his life? Surely if that had been me, I would have had a hard time leaving him. He . . . he didn't. He left and he made a life here. So quickly."

I felt guilty even saying all this. Should I be complaining that he didn't sit and pine for me?

"I wanted him to live his life, but I expected him to at least have held out some hope that I would join him like we'd planned. He didn't. He was having sex with Cat. It didn't take him long."

Slate didn't respond right away. I didn't expect him to. What was he supposed to say to this? "I'm sorry"? There was no response he could give me to make it better.

"Tonight we were at a party. He had this life, and these friends who didn't even know who I was. I didn't fit, and he didn't seem to notice or care. He wanted me to sit there beside him while he laughed and had a good time. That wasn't what we were always like. I used to at least know his friends, and I wasn't as lost. But I've realized that he had always been the center of attention and he expected me to just fall into place at his side. I don't want that anymore."

Slate pulled his Jeep down a dirt road. Normally this would seem strange, but I trusted Slate. That was something else I didn't understand. Why did I trust him so completely?

We were stopped under a clear night sky in a field filled with grass and wildflowers. I wondered if he had brought many girls out here for something completely different. It was a beautiful spot, though.

"Crawford will regret this one day," Slate said as he turned his body toward me. "He had you. He'd lived a perfect life with you and he didn't even know what he had because he hadn't tried anything else. Me . . . well, I've tried it all. I'm not wondering what's on the other side. I've been there, and it is lonely. He'll realize it one day, and it'll be too late."

That was sweet and I appreciated him saying it, but I didn't want Crawford to regret anything. I wanted him to be happy.

"Couples go to college and grow apart every day," I said. "Before my coma, I think the idea of this would have broken me.

But it all changed while I was asleep. I found a part of me I didn't know was missing. What hurts is he cheated so easily and so soon."

Slate leaned forward and cupped my face with his hand. It felt familiar and exciting all at once. "When you were sleeping and I would read to you and talk to you, I felt something. Hell, maybe it was your face, because you have an exceptional one. But I felt a connection. I'd never had that before, and I made excuses to see you by bringing your family coffee. Sure, I'm a nice guy and I wanted to help out, but in reality I couldn't imagine a guy not standing by your side, holding your hand, praying you would wake up. I . . ." He paused and leaned close to me. His scent made my body tingle. ". . . Just knew there was something special there. Then you woke up and I was right. You went to see my uncle D because you cared about an old man you didn't know. You stood by me as he died. You cared. No girl has ever cared before, Vale."

Tears stung my eyes. Slate was so much more than he was given credit for. I leaned into his hand and closed my eyes. Instead of the safe feeling I had with Crawford, my pulse raced with Slate. He made the world brighter and full of the unknown.

"I had to be sure," I told him, opening my eyes to lock with his gaze. "I had to know what I had with Crawford was over. He was all I'd known."

Slate dropped his hand, and I felt cold without his touch.

"I know. You still need time. Twelve years is a long time to love someone. Moving on can't happen overnight. But when you're ready, you know where to find me."

As much as I wanted Slate to pull me into his arms and kiss me, I knew he was right. There had to be closure with Crawford.

"Thank you," I said, wishing there were words that meant more, that expressed what I was feeling.

"For what?"

I looked at his beautiful face and those eyes that seemed to haunt my dreams. "For being you."

Slate chuckled. "I've never been thanked for that before."

I smiled at his amusement. "How will I know?" I asked him.

"Your heart will," he replied.

CHAPTER FIFTY-FIVE

VALE

CRAWFORD WAS IN my dorm room when I returned that night. He cried and admitted to sleeping with Cat as well as two other girls. He blamed it on being lost without me and acting out in pain. He begged me to forgive him.

I let him say all he had to say, then told him the truth. I didn't love him anymore. From the moment I opened my eyes, things had been different. We couldn't go back because we had both changed. I could forgive him for the girls, but I'd never forget it. My heart was closed to him now. I wanted him happy, but not with me.

He had cried more and blamed himself for not staying with me. For listening to his mother and leaving when it was time. I let him talk and listened, although I was aware that he had to work through this on his own.

When I watched him finally leave, he asked me if there was a chance for us one day. I told him the truth. No. We were the past and our story was a big part of both of us. But it was over now. Our futures held different things.

Not once did I cry—or even feel like crying. Seeing his tears didn't make me feel vindicated. It was just sad that this was how it all ended. All our plans for the future were no longer important. They were the dreams of children. Children who were growing up.

AFTER HE WAS gone, I called Knox and told him I had ended things. I left out the girls because Knox wouldn't forgive him for that. He'd go after him and they'd both end up in jail or the hospital. I needed my brother and my family to understand that I wanted more. I wanted a life that *I* got to plan.

Over the next month, I focused on work and school. I didn't go out. I was alone most of the time, but I was content. Knox forced me to eat with him some and I went home twice for family dinners so everyone could see I was smiling. I was happy. I wasn't lost and sad.

It was almost November when I looked up from the coffee-maker at work to see Slate walk in. He hadn't been by since the night he picked me up on the road. He hadn't texted and he hadn't called. I had seen him only three times from a distance, and each time he didn't see me and had been alone, too.

I was getting off work in five minutes. It was a Sunday and tomorrow was Halloween. We had been busy all week with the specialty coffee drinks that were about to change for Thanksgiving.

"Hey," I said, feeling my face flush from excitement. Just seeing him this close and being able to smell him made me happy.

"Hey," he replied as a smile curled up one corner of his mouth.

"How . . . how are you?" I asked nervously.

"Missing you," he replied.

My chest tightened and my heart soared. He had missed me. I had lain in bed many nights telling myself I didn't need a man to make me happy. I would find happiness inside me. However, it never made me not miss him. Wonder about him.

"Good," I replied, untying my apron.

"Good?" he asked, still smiling.

I nodded and tossed my apron in the dirty linen basket. "I'm gone, Jake," I called out to the new guy we'd hired last month. I was training him, but he had this. And if not, what better day than today to let him figure it out?

"Shift over?" Slate asked as I walked around the counter toward him.

"Yes," I replied.

"Do you have plans?"

I nodded. "Yes."

He looked deflated. "Oh."

Then I stepped closer to him and put my palms on his chest as I stood on my tiptoes and covered his mouth with mine. This was what I had been dreaming about. Being near him. Being able to kiss him. Being able to know that he was there and life was going to be full of excitement and new things.

His hands found my face and he held it gently as he deepened the kiss. I slid my hands up his chest and wrapped them around his neck as his mint-flavored breath mingled with mine. I don't know how much time passed before I finally pulled back and inhaled deeply to catch my breath.

"This. This is my plan," I told him breathlessly.

He grinned. "Then I'm the luckiest fucker on the planet."

Thank you for reading this Feiwel and Friends book.

The friends who made **AS SHE FADES** possible are:

JEAN FEIWEL, Publisher

LIZ SZABLA, Associate Publisher

RICH DEAS, Senior Creative Director

HOLLY WEST, Editor

ANNA ROBERTO, Editor

CHRISTINE BARCELLONA, Editor

KAT BRZOZOWSKI, Editor

ALEXEI ESIKOFF, Senior Managing Editor

KIM WAYMER, Senior Production Manager

ANNA POON, Assistant Editor

EMILY SETTLE, Administrative Assistant

DANIELLE MAZZELLA DI BOSCO, Senior Designer

MELINDA ACKELL, Copy Chief

Follow us on Facebook or visit us online at mackids.com.
Our books are friends for life.